Salt of the Earth

A Collection of Short Stories

By A. A. J. Metcalf

Preface

Every person is an individual and each chooses to live their own life. The stories in this book are all different, as are the characters in them. There are close relationships like John and Joan's, Bob and Meg's or like Jack and Jill's which stumble on. There are stories of joy and happiness, but sadness for some. Many good people appear in stories that are joyous and others that contain characters that do wrong, most of which reap what they have sown. All together there is a varied landscape of people and places, showing the variety of humankind, bringing thoughtful emotions, feeling, and reactions

Contents

Horace & Evelyn

"Get in the car NOW, WE'RE GOING TO Asda to get Chubby Brown's DVD for Christmas". Evelyn did as she was told, she had done for the last seventeen years; ever since she married that ignorant man. Horace, an unpleasant self-centred boastful man, who often totally ignored his belittled wife.

Sitting at a table in the supermarket café, Horace tucked into his big breakfast, with extra chips and two buttered barm cakes. On the table next to theirs sat a family, mum, dad, and three children. Looking at their old clothes and demeanour, and sharing two plates of chips and beans between, it was clear to see they were very poor, although all of them appeared to be clean and tidy. When they had finished eating and their plates were as clean as if washed, they made their way out of the café. A few minutes later Evelyn spied a piece of paper under the table where they had been sitting.

When hungry Horace brought back his pudding, spotted Richard with custard, Evelyn showed him the paper, a lottery ticket, that the poor father must have dropped. "I'm going after them" Evelyn said but, looking out of the window Horace remarked, "TOO LATE, they've just got on the Farnworth bus, the ticket is OURS".

The following Thursday evening Horace checked his own five Lucky Dips. "No bloody good, four numbers out of thirty". Angrily he threw them in the bin. That lucky dip we picked up in Asda, I checked it last night and put it in the bin said Evelyn. Evelyn had checked the ticket, put it in the bin but, never let go of the ticket that was worth £3.7 million. Something deep inside Evelyn was stirring, she felt her spirits lifting and her will strengthening.

She now had an urgent mission to find the true millionaires.

The following Sunday saw Horace and Evelyn in the same café. There was no sign of the lotto family, then, ten minutes later the family sat down in the opposite corner of the café. Evelyn was on pins nervously anticipating when she could show the family the ticket.

Horace went to the food counter for his pudding. Evelyn with an eye on Horace tells the parents of the lucky family the fantastic news, and 'phone numbers are exchanged. Evelyn returns to Horace who is up to his eyeballs with sticky toffee pudding. I'm leaving you Horace, I'll be at my mother's where my things have been taken this morning". Horace open mouthed with sticky toffee pudding and custard dripping down his face is bewildered. Minutes later as he looks out of the window, he sees Evelyn close the door on the taxi she has entered.

Christmas day finds Evelyn half a million pounds richer, dining and enjoying festive cheer with the lucky Smith family, at Evelyn's parents' house.

A pitiful lonely Horace sits amidst empty take-away boxes and beer bottles in his parlour. He opens the Christmas card from Evelyn, reads the attached letter, and then looks with amazement at the sum of money that is wrote on a cheque in his name.

Well it is the season of good will—the amount on the cheque—I'll leave you to write that on!

A Pleasant Evening

On the Thursday of the sunniest calmest week of Summer, we drove down an unmade track, leaving a trail of dust that covered the following long base land rover. The occupant of that vehicle disembarked; he had a dusty complexion, and matching beard and hair. He introduced himself as our pilot for the evening.

We all rallied round to help: we put the large latticed wicker basket on its side, and then everyone; the pilot, his three able and experienced helpers, along with SIXTEEN expectant and excited individuals helped to spread the gigantic area of the red sheet out on the ground. Gradually the red material rose up, as it filled with air and pulled the wicker basket upright.

The pilot, who had taught us beforehand, shouted the instruction for us to get in our allocated places in the balloon. We scrambled over the side, and helped some of the older people to get in. Immediately our wicker carriage moved along the ground, it was like a vehicle without wheels. Then----The next second, we were all peering down at the ever-diminishing ground. Twenty feet-Fifty Feet-One hundred feet, and finally rising up to Two Thousand feet.

We raised our eyes to look around at the magnificent panorama: Blackpool Tower to the south west, the mountains of the Lake District to the North West. Hills. Fields, Streams. Little patches that were villages, Fantastic!

After ten minutes the pilot took us down to 100 feet and lower. The great thing was we were only travelling at 10mph: So SLOW and so SILENT. Cruising along now, we brushed the top of trees with the basket. Then the pilot chose an alleyway between two mature spreading splendiferous oak trees. Below now appeared what looked like Toy Town. Set out like a model village was Kirby Lonsdale.

We skimmed over the meandering River Lune, and saw it disappearing in the distance. The patchwork quilt of the fields, some looking like green felt or golden silk, others like lace. Farmers on tractors creating beautiful artwork, a living tapestry; our heritage created by man.

Fields of sheep scattered when they saw the enormous pendulous object. Cows stood still, each looking like a china ornament. Then suddenly, at the same instant, as one unit, all the cattle ran together towards the balloon, did they think it was delivering them food?

We journeyed onwards to where no livestock roamed and landed softly at 2mph.We helped to tuck the red material into a large black bag. Then we sipped our champagne as the descending sun hit the top of the hills and sent glistening golden light spreading out to a great distance, and a streak of white light ran down over the green valley. What a beautiful end to our fascinating experience.

Avril's Night

It was all going so well; here we were at the annual New Year's Eve Party. It was cold and icy outside but, warm and welcoming inside. Us men, us uncles, Roy, Gary, Wayne Glen and Chris who's house it is, were in the kitchen dad dancing to some old soul numbers. Oh, and of course mad uncle Norbert, who this year had been told by many, not least his devoted wife Julie, to behave himself. We had already witnessed Norbert annually strip out of his shirt and trousers, which he'd change in an upstairs bedroom, stroll downstairs and saunter through the packed rooms, in a mankini, budgie smugglers, apron with no back , or in full attire as a Scotsman, with beard, wig and hat, stockings, sporran, and kilt which he'd gaily lift up now and again to show off the appendage that was sewn under the kilt. Apart from these episodes it was great to see Norbert who had an infectious laugh and got everyone in a good party mood.

This year Norbert promised he would be good, there were more younger children present, so he only had the clothes he came in. We were all having a great time when Avril, a very shy, nervous, plain type of girl, dressed in red polo neck jumper and blue pleated skirt, with a piece of holly in her hair, and silver tinsel around her waist, was on route from the lounge to see the crowd outside, when uncle Norbert, who was a chunky well-built fella, seized hold of Avril. He first of all jived to and fro, then twisted Avril around 360degrees, throwing her at tangents across the kitchen, and pulling her vigorously back to him. The next record was Michael Jackson's, "The way you make me feel", a favourite of Norbert's. He picked Avril up, squeezing her hard around the waist and swinging her round and round, twisting and reeling. Then with unbelievable strength, one hand at the top of her back and the other on her low back, he hoisted her up above his head shouting, "Let's spin Avril into 2018". And that is just what he did. Norbert twisted, spinning round and round with Avril like a rag doll, until he was so dizzy he started to stumble. Yet he managed a final almighty push, just as uncle Roy was re-entering the kitchen via the back door, and Avril was launched from Norbert like a cruise missile. Myself and the four uncles standing in line, watched the trajectory fly through the air, out through the open door.

Luckily for Avril she caught her body on the door casing, and this flipped her up straight. She landed on her feet but, with her weight on her right leg. The uncles and I watched Avril in slow motion as she slid past the kitchen window, then she turned right at the gable end of the house and disappeared from our view. As she hit the incline of the icy flag paving, we could hear her shouting "aaaaaaahhhhhhhaaa!" We rushed out of the kitchen, through the lounge and out of the front door faster than Usain Bolt, to see Avril grab a concrete fencing post, only to be flicked up into the air, pirouetting and then turn majestically and land back on her feet, only to continue down six flights of steps towards the open garden gate....Meanwhile cousin Dean had parked his car but, he had hit the ice coming down the hill at a tangent from Avril's run. In an effort to stop, Dean grabbed Avril's arm and pulled on it, only to shoot her momentarily up the slope, she then turned, slipped on her back, and feet first slid under Dean's legs. Dean grabbed Avril's hands. Dean then slipped and landed on his bottom behind Avril, with his legs to her sides. They slid down another twenty yards and came to an abrupt stop. There was a thunderous clapping and cheering, not just from the fifty people at our party, but the whole of the close who had shot out of their houses when they heard the piercing cry of Avril. Then, as if by magic, right on cue, the local church bells started chiming in the new year. Fireworks were shooting into the air, and the full crystal moon shone down on the iridescent icy winter scene.

Avril and Dean embraced and kissed. That night Avril didn't feel the pain of her bumps and bruises. They had helped her not only to find new confidence and courage but, a true love in Dean.

Avril and Dean married in March that year, and their first child is due…………

I bet you can guess when! Yes, on the 31st December, New Year's Eve.

Bob & Meg

It's the mid-fifties. In the mill town of Notbowl in Upper Lever, in a house in the middle of a long row of houses lives Bob the eldest surviving son of dad Bob and mum Annie. Mum altogether giving birth to thirteen children in the two-bedroom house. The bathroom and toilet were divided off with T&G floorboards, nailed onto a wooden framework, courtesy of Bob's father, which gave the family another bedroom. Bob the senior was a hardworking man, stuck in the local tannery for five and a half days. Later along with the tannery work, and with the family growing year by year, he started playing drums for a jazz band in the local clubs.

Young Bob was an honest lad who would help his father in many ways; often when dad came home late from work and was rather inebriated. Young Bob would help to put the evening meal on the table, dad getting the best of what they had to eat. By the time there were eight or more at the table, there would be only little pickings left for the kids and mother. A loaf of bread was sliced by mother, then a slice sparsely margarined by dad at the head of the table who then threw the slice through the air, where it usually landed on the table and slid towards one of his children. It was like dad was practicing being a croupier, throwing cards down a table in the casino for the game of blackjack, only dad's pieces of bread were faster and airborne longer than any playing cards.

Young Bob was a great help to his mother. When a baby was due, he'd fuss around mum, wiping her face and neck with a cold flannel, (face cloth). He'd wash her feet, legs and arms to comfort her. Standing upright both mother and son's legs would be shaking in unison as they walked with the midwife towards the bedroom. Young Bob brought whatever the midwife needed, then left the room shutting the door behind him. Other kid's birth's varied, sometimes it was a race two streets down to "Aunty Mabel's" - no relation, but besides having the only television in the area, they also had the only telephone to call the ambulance.

Bob still played out in the street whenever he could. A dozen or more kids would be playing various games; the boys cowboys and Indians, tag, football with a pig's bladder. The girls skipping, hopscotch, spin top and older kids kiss catch. There were lots of friends around and also school mates.

As Bob grew into his teens, he was found more with his own age group of friends.. . There was a lot of, "adult", conversations, or so the wise young people thought, yet still time for kiss catch or, "dare". Bob took a liking to a girl called Elizabeth who lived in the larger house built on the end of the row. One summer's day, Elizabeth's parents were out of the house for a few hours. Elizabeth invited young Bob into her house. Bob could not believe how beautiful and modern everything was. "You are so lucky to have all this", Bob said. Elizabeth replied, "But unlucky not to have any brothers or sisters like you". She walked over to Bob who was thirteen at the time, and without a word pulled Bob's shorts down, and then lifted her short summer dress and pulled her knickers down. Bob looked down at his, and then across at hers, pulled his shorts up, said, "Mum's calling us in, see you later". He exited quickly and ran back up the street to enjoy a game of marbles with two of his younger brothers.

Bob and Elizabeth now called Meg by all her friends, went to different schools. They hung around in the same gang but weren't united as a couple till they were both sixteen. Bob was working as an apprentice engineer and Meg was at the local college. They spent many happy days together. They swam twice a week at the local Low Street baths, walked home, hand in hand, sharing a hot Vimto. They went to the local picture house, one of a dozen in the town which some years ago had boasted thirty cinemas. If one of Bob's brothers or sisters, or a friend, asked him to tell them about the film, he'd have to say it was okay or make something up. Bob never took in much of the film, he spent the majority of the time looking at Meg. At times he'd squeeze Meg's hand, whereupon she would look at Bob, give him a smile, and then turn back to watch the film. His mates had said to Bob, "Do you get on the double seats on the back row when you're at the flicks? it all goes on there". Bob would just answer, "There's enough going on half a dozen rows from the back". "Woooooooo you lucky dog Bob".

All was going well. Bob and Meg saw each other for the next twelve months. The swimming had ceased, now it was the "pictures" on a Sunday evening. They met once a week for a walk, or if it was pouring rain they went for a drink in the temperance bar, tea and biscuits as they chatted together.

On their walks, or more so in the, "café", the talk was about their work. Bob recalling each minute detail and effort of his work on the bench or lathe. He certainly gave Meg a clear insight into all the intricacies of his engineering career. Meg listened in the main to Bob, saying the odd, "OH", or, "Yes that's right!", or, "Yes that's interesting". When Bob was eventually winding down and lifting his cup of tea up to his mouth, she with bated breath would forcibly open with the latest incident or occurrence that had come about at college or tell a tale that she'd heard from her parents or others in college or on the street. Bob wasn't keen on gossip. If the talk was of a serious nature, only then would he take it all in. Even though Meg was a clever girl and very studious at her work, she still took life very lightly. She was carefree and enjoying her teenage years. On Saturday nights Meg would be in town with her old girlfriends from school, downing a couple of gin and its, chatting, laughing and dancing the night away. Meg was slim built, of medium height with good looks and an easy-going nature with a natural smile. She was asked out by young men on many occasions, but always answered, "I have a boyfriend". To Meg at her age Bob was a "Friend", and nothing to get serious about. Along with having known him for years, she did admire his honesty, his commitment to work and love for his family. Yet with all the good characteristics Bob had, to Meg it stayed on the level of good companionship. She respected Bob and knew he would make a good husband and father, for someone, but any thoughts or feelings that it might be her never entered into her mind or touched her heart or soul.

Whether it was Bob's upbringing, he was the eldest child of the family, the responsibilities of that, which gave him a genuine care for all, along with that serious bent he possessed, he felt a love for Meg that was different from the love he had for family. In his head he had always had "something" for Meg. She had always been a friend, a mate, someone he could talk to, and tell her things that he would never discuss with his brothers, sisters or even his mates. Even though they had a kiss on the cheek at times, it never went any further. Bob had so much respect for Meg. When he was with Meg any cares or worries left him, and he felt truly happy. His heart at times beating as loud and fast as when he'd ran all the way up Charley Old Road, a steep incline, to see his mate John who lived near Toffcocker Pond. Bob was filled with love for Meg. When he was alone his thoughts were about Meg, he looked forward to seeing her on the days in between their meetings. He felt sure they would start to see each other more often, and he day dreamed they would be together for ever.

While walking round Brownhills reservoir one sunny Sunday afternoon in the month of May, Bob asked Meg," Shall we start seeing each other one night in the week, maybe Friday?". Meg was taken aback. They both stopped, turned to look into each other's faces. There was a stony silence for a minute, then Meg gathering her thoughts said, "I have all my college work, I see my old friends Saturday, like you when you go out with your mates or brothers. I feel Sundays are the only times right now. Most Sundays we at least see each other for a couple of hours in the afternoon, and usually see each other in the evening". Bob looked disappointed, "We'll carry on then, we can see each other more when you have your breaks from college. Let's just enjoy our walk now Bob. How is your new little sister coming on, she must be a few months old now"? As they walked on Bob replied, "She's four months this Tuesday, she's so good, smiles most of the time and has started to do loud noises, screeches and…" Meg was miles away. She'd never thought of the future - her focus was to do well at college. The time with bob was nice, the walks, the talks, a quieter time. The Saturday nights with the girls was a time to completely forget College work. Sundays had become just that easy routine, a return to normality before it was back to college the next day. In Meg's mind she'd always thought Bob would meet someone in that special way, maybe in a year or two. For herself, she was off to university soon, to get a good degree, and then to do well in her career. The thought of marriage or babies had never entered her head. She was only eighteen years of age. Meg was mature and intelligent in many ways. Some would say she was a free spirit, some might say she was selfish. Meg felt she had something to prove, she was the only one in her street, the only one of five in her year at college who was going on to university. She was an only child, she had the drive and ambition, helped by her parents to build herself a good life, to live comfortably, free from any financial worries.

The week after that Sunday Bob still thought that he and Meg would gradually start to see each other more. Summer time we can start to go places, catch the train to the seaside, Westport, Lightpool, or go the Lakes, great! It all takes time and Bob had the patience to let the relationship grow into the time when he would ask her to marry him, in a year or two, when they were both twenty. Bob went about his work happily, thinking everything was continuing right for him and Meg. Some would say Bob was too innocent, too naïve to not realise that the fulfilment of his desires would never be reached. When Bob first started to see Meg, his mates looked up to him, "You've got a fantastic bird there, good looking, she's really fit!" However, as the years passed, his mates talked of Bob and Meg's relationship between themselves, where was it going if anywhere? She was out of his class, yet they still stuck together, though that was usually only on Sundays. Perhaps it would all be good, opposites attract and all that. Bob's mates asked how it was going and, "You're both keen then?". Two of Bob's mates Dick and Tony had both managed or mismanaged to put their girlfriends in the pudding club, "Up the duff", as they said, and now both were married. Each couple, now family were living in rented accommodation. They seemed happy, yet both of them were taking life more serious now. Saturday nights out had turned to Fridays now, due to married couples having Saturday nights out together. Dick and Tony turned out now and again on Fridays, lad's night out was changing rapidly!

At the age of twenty-one both Bob and Meg had a feather in their caps. Meg gained a first-class degree in Business and Marketing and applied for jobs in England and abroad. Bob had left the engineering game eighteen months earlier and got a job with Japanese car giant Nisoto. He worked partly on sales and also in the service section. Within six months he was in charge of the parts department. After seventeen months he got the position of assistant manager of the site.

Bob and Meg now met for a meal on Sunday, or occasionally on a Friday with an old mate of Bob's from their apprentice days. George was now on his third house renovation, the first two homes rented out in good areas. George was with his girlfriend Kath, who worked on one of the cosmetic counters in Bedenhams store in town. Bob and Meg now met most Sunday mornings for a walk. They both had good walking gear, so they ventured over South West Pennine Moor area, or up to the lakes. They never had a stopover for the night, Bob would suggest one but Meg, for one reason or another, had always to return home. After various talks over many weeks the previous year, both Bob and Meg had fully disclosed how they felt about each other, and what they wanted for the next few years and beyond. They both enjoyed the time with George and Kath, they got on together very well. Even though George and Kath's relationship appeared rather platonic, they were both very happy on their dates out.

Meg had been interviewed for a position in Sydney Australia. She attended the interview in London. A few weeks later she received a letter asking her to go to Australia house in Manchester. Three months later, after all the paperwork and 'phone calls, she had the plane tickets in her hand. It wasn't such a big deal for Meg. For years she'd read up on Australia in the local library. Two of her old school mates had backpacked around Asia and then worked in Aussie for a while. The two girls had returned home but, Trish had met an Aussie fella named Rob, and returned to Aussie within weeks. Meg passed through the emigration quickly, due to her having the papers to say she had a job in Aussie and somewhere to stay, in Rob's house of course. Also, Meg had money transferred to a bank account in Sydney. So, Meg was off to Rob and Trish's house in Dee Why on the northern side of Sydney. The company that Meg would work for was in Manly, just a few miles from Rob and Trish's home.

One of the secretaries in Bob's workplace had taken his eye, and they'd become very friendly. Deidre was nine years older than Bob and had three children. It was a month after Deidre's divorce when they first went together for an evening meal out. After meg's departure things had developed quickly on all fronts, they announced the date of their marriage in six months' time.

There were sad farewells for Meg to her mother and father, to her friends, and of course to such a close friend that Bob had become to her; from playing as a child in the streets together, to a true bonding of friendship through their teenage years into their early twenties. However, with all that had happened in Meg's life she knew she had to make a new life for herself.

Nineteen years later Meg was working in the city of Sydney. She had a high-powered job with the pay to match. Her mum and dad had moved from Notbowl to Higham and St. Hilda's, a lovely seaside town on the west coast, soon after Meg had gone to Australia. Meg's mother was ill, she had a stroke and was bed ridden. Meg, "Tore her hair out", for three months deciding whether to have time off work and go to mums for a visit, or to give up her good life in Australia, possibly forever, and do all she could for her parents, after all she was their only child. She had never been back to England. Just as she knew twenty or so years ago that she had to make a new life for herself, now she knew she had to return to her parents, return to home. In her heart she wanted to return to her parents, and to have a major change of job and lifestyle.

With all the hard work and long hours of the last twenty years, Meg was easily able to afford the small terraced house she bought in Higham, a short walk from her parents' home. For twelve months she helped her parents whenever she could. Her mother died twelve months later. Meg did most of the funeral arrangements, under the instruction of her still very capable father.

Meg worked for a local building firm, three days a week, doing their secretarial and accounting work. Meg had helped her parents from the day she arrived back from Australia, unfortunately her mother died twelve months later. Meg did most of the funeral arrangements, under the clear instructions from her still very capable father.

Throughout her life in Australia Meg had often thought of Bob. As the years rolled on she wondered why they hadn't become a couple. She knew now it was because of herself, wanting to be by herself. Yes, she thought, it was selfish of me, and I left the person closest to me. Since arriving back in England she had thought about Bob a lot. She was sure he would have married and had children. Oh yes, he would make a good husband and father. There was something in Meg's heart that was drawing her to find out how he was, and hopefully meet him.

Meg's mum's funeral was in Higham, many people who knew them attended. Meg thought she recognised a party of four from Notbowl. After the meal in the Higham Beach Restaurant, Meg walked over to them. "Hello Meg, sorry we see each other after all these years on such a sad occasion". It was Betty, who had been in the same class as Meg throughout school. Betty introduced Meg to her husband Cliff and then said, "You'll remember John and Beryl, they were in the year above us". The five of them sat down at a table in the next room and ordered their drinks. The talk was all about schooldays and the dance hall days. Suddenly Betty said, "It was such a shock, a real shame to hear about Bob". "WHAT? What happened", said Meg, I've not heard anything about Bob since I emigrated to Australia twenty years ago". There was an awkward silence for thirty seconds, then Betty said, "You won't know he married a lady, a divorcee, who was ten years older than him and had three children of her own. That was about a year after you left. I believe he became a good husband and did all he could for the children". "So, he's happily married then?" Meg quietly asked. "This is the story most of us heard Meg". Meg took a sip of her dry white wine, and the others took a sip of their drinks. "You'll remember Bob had a bicycle, well he bought a racing bike, pedal bike not motor bike, so he joined the local clarion club. He'd be off up the A6 to Harton, or even to the Lakes with the lads. It seemed they were a friendly bunch, but the story is he got too friendly with one particular chap. They say he'd cycle to Worwich on a different day than clarion days to the house where the chap lived by himself. People then spread rumours about the pair, which reached his daughter Gemma who told her mother". Beryl interrupted Betty and said, "They were divorced the year after that, Bob ended up in a flat on Fromwich Street. In that day it was all prostitutes and druggies, it seemed with all the stress he lost his job, he did work at Cosda supermarket after. "Do you know where he is now?" Meg asked. The four were still for a full minute, their facial expressions changed to those of pity, they all looked up and stared at meg, their lips shut tight, then with an intake of breath, their mouths opened, and they exhaled the air in a simultaneous sigh. Betty placed her hand on Megs, and began to speak in a quieter tone, "As Beryl said, he was working at Cosda. The one at Bastler Bridge in Notbowl. The report in the paper said he was driving a fork lift truck which extended to its height to pick a pallet of off the top shelf in the warehouse. It said the truck hinged forward and then back, giving Bob whiplash and two fractured vertebrae in the middle of his back where he had hit the back of the fork lift seat. "Oh my God", Meg held her two hands to her face. "Then it appears the forks dropped with the load and poor Bob was thrown forward, when his head hit the steel girder it killed him outright". "Yes", John spoke for the first time, "The only good thing to come out of it was that his own family got a big pay out from Cosda". Meg was ashen, she couldn't speak. After five minutes of what seemed gossip from the four, Meg asked, "Where was Bob's funeral, where was he buried?" "He'd started attending the little church at Stremington, the village above Worwich. Me and Cliff went to the funeral, it was just beautiful." So he's buried there?", interrupted Meg. "Yes, he's buried in St. John's churchyard".

This was such a sad end for Bob, and it looked like a sad end for Meg the spinster, who seemed destined never to marry.

The Saturday after Meg's mother's funeral, Meg picked Dad up in her car. They threw some of mum's ashes into the sea at Higham, scattered some at Farnside Knot, one of her mum's favourite walks. The last remaining ashes were to be scattered on Stremington Pike, the walk and views which the family enjoyed so much when they lived in Notbowl. After lunch at Farnside, her father asked, "Are you going to Stremington now?". "Yes, we said we'd do all three on the same day". "Well you must go by yourself and have the memories of you and mum together. I am ready to go back to Higham now". "I'll go tomorrow with them dad". "Get it done today Meg, it seems the right time".

Meg took dad back home, then joined the motorway route to Warwich, some forty minutes' drive, and another ten to Stremington. She parked her car near the gate at the bottom of the hill and carried the urn with the remaining ashes up to the top of the pike. Stood alone at the top she held the urn, closed her eyes and a beautiful quietness came over her, with the feeling that mum was around. She opened her eyes, after what seemed an endless time, and the view before her came to life. All the colours in the panoramic view before her were of the clearest, deepest and most iridescent she had witnessed in all her life. Great joy filled her heart, and she waved the urn left and right, the ashes disappearing into the heaven before and around her.

Meg slowly made the descent and got into her car. She drove the short distance to the centre of the village, parked the car near the little church gate, entered the church yard, and made her way past the church to the graveyard. It looked easy to find the plot, in the far right-hand corner Meg could see where all the recent burials were. There was a man kneeling down at the foot of one of the graves. Meg passed the grave with the man's back to her, looked at the cross at the head of the grave and all the flowers and cards.

Meg thought she made out the name Bob on one of the cards, and then saw the word B-O-B. in flowers near the cross. Meg decided to go back to her car and come back a little later. She thought the man kneeling was perhaps his friend from Warwich, or one of his brothers. As Meg turned away from the grave, the man turned his head to look at the person who'd stopped for those few seconds behind him. Then he recognised the person and shouted, "Meg". Meg looked back at him. "It's George Meg, come back, I'll leave you here and, "No.. No please don't go George." "I'll come back in five minutes or so Meg". George then went around to the front of the church. Meg fell to her knees on the dry ground were

Ground were George had left his imprint. Meg's tears rolled down her cheeks, she sobbed and sobbed. George looked round the side of the church, and quickly retreated back to the front. Meg placed three red roses on the pile of flowers. She prayed for her dear friend, her love. A rose from her, and the other two for Bob and the love he had found after his marriage break-up. She looked to the temporary wooden cross, remembering all the happy times they had spent together. She felt a clearness of mind. A serene smile came upon her face, she knew that Bob was happy, all was well.

Meg walked slowly to the front of the church. "All is right", Meg said. "Yes, all IS right", George echoed. The two of them hugged each other, holding each other hard against the other, and then tenderly embracing. After five minutes they looked at each other, and their eyes melted, their hearts quickened, and they again hugged each other tightly. Ten minutes later they were sharing coffee and cake in the little village tea room. Both gave a brief overview of their last twenty years. Meg never having a serious friendship, and George? "What about Kath who worked at Bedhamans?" Meg asked." Kath met a chap twenty-five year older than her, and went on to live the life of Riley, without a care or worry, well for many years, till the money started to run out. I've always remained single".

Here they were then, happy as two single teenagers together, yet with the wisdom that the last twenty years had brought to them.

Six months later Meg and George were married. Another two years later they could be seen pushing a pram. The baby had been christened in St. John's and named Robert. Mother and Father calling their precious child, Baby Bobby.

A Million Happy Memories

When I was a young boy I lived and worked with my best friend on a farm. He was a strong as an ox and had the courage of a lion. He was an astute and wise man, who taught me many good things in work and in life. He had a heart as big as the moon and goodness and righteousness shone from him, like the brilliance of the noon day summer sun. The fullness of heart, clear mind and pure spirit would shine onto his countenance. His whole face would light up, and the most beautiful light blue eyes, full of joy, bliss and happiness would penetrate your very soul.

As a little child we would run after and pick up a runaway hen or a white haired pink piglet. We'd charge through the bluebell wood in springtime and gather in the summer hay under the scorching July sun. Winter time saw us clearing away the pure pristine glistening snow. Then we would smash the ice below to reveal the jet-black cobble stones in front of our farm house. In the ice-cold shippan we'd deliver new born struggling calves from their mothers.

One December saw my creative friend; who seemed able to make anything from a large cabin/shed to a small jewellery box in wood, spending long hours making me a wooden fort for Christmas, so that I could play with my soldiers, some of them made of lead. Another Christmas I got a wooden garage with real petrol pumps and ramps, where I drove my corgi or dinky cars in for their service. Always great presents, apart from one Christmas when I was eleven years of age, a disappointment, I was told Rachael Welch would not fit into my Santa sack.

As the years passed, anniversaries, birthdays, family holidays and get-togethers, and always at Christmas the house lit up trimmed with decorations, the pine tree resplendent with wrapped presents, gifts laid underneath. Boxing day was his birthday and great fun was enjoyed at his party. Some years later in our lives we'd enjoy a quieter occasion and go for a meal to a restaurant.

It was he who drove me to the railway station on-route to emigrate to Australia (in 1972). Some years later on arriving back at Manchester Piccadilly, on a late December afternoon that was wet, cold, dark and dismal, I looked around for him, and saw an old man push his way through the large crowd. Bent over through life's hard work and hardship, (about the age I am now 68), he slowly came forward out of the darkness, and unashamedly, with that undying love, hugged, embraced, and showered me with words of devotion.

Lately I'd visit, or take down to the market, this man who had given me so much in life. Any cares or worries I had at the time would evaporate as we chatted together.

This great man from the countryside, who was deeply saddened with the demise of this once great glorious green and pleasant land, still inspired in me strength and courage. The qualities so abundantly evident in his own self, along with that enviable devotion, true sense of his own purpose and unending duty in life. These qualities present on November the third this year; when with all the family holding him, our dad cast off his mortal coil and very easily and peacefully passed onto his new life.

Christmas may never be the same without parents, we have been so blessed and happy. If you still have parents, do everything you can for them, just like they have done for you. After they are gone from this world you will have been truly blessed and given a million happy memories.

The Sparefellows

Susie went to the N.N.T.C. ,(Notbowl Natural Treatment Centre), for some relief for her aching back. Susie's a small lady with a low back that curves right in, (Exaggerated

Lordosis), the middle of her back hunches the other way backwards, (Kyphosis), and her neck and head are pushed forward, so her head meets you before her body. She may be age seventy-nine but is hoping the therapist can straighten her posture so that she can keep up her thrice weekly ballroom dancing.

Susie was sitting on the couch while her neck was being treated, with the therapist behind her. She asked, "Are you a Sparefellow?" The therapist was more than a little taken aback, and unsure of just what she meant. "Well my WIFE says I am a little odd, why Susie? "NO", Susie replies, "Are you a member of the Sparefellows?" The therapist scratched his head, "No, I'm a member of the Osteomyologists, fully paid up and insured". A third "NO" from Susie. "You've heard of the Masons?"- "Ohooo yes"- "The buffaloes", "Ah yes they meet in the top room of The Top Kicker public house in Ramsdale, but I know nothing about them". Susie explained, "The Sparefellows are a group of people who raise money for local charities, their Lodge, ---a bemused look from the Osteo chap------is in Back Dark Street, only one hundred yards from here". She continued, "It's only twenty pounds to join and you get ten pounds back to spend in any store in town. With your membership you can attend all their social evenings or events, like last night's ten pin bowling, crown green bowling in the summer, or many days out to various places of interest. The inaugural grand masters night, ----even more bemusement----is at Brownhills hall, with free dinner and drinks. And......all your dentist, optician and doctors' fees are free, unbelievable but true". It still didn't grab the Osteo, "That's great for you Susie". At that time, he didn't know Susie received £10 every time she enlisted someone, but…. He was sure £20 was coming her way when she threw him the irresistible incentive, the final bait. "At the socials", she said, "Wine is only ten pence a glass and cans of beer fifty pence". The Osteo snatched the forms out of her hand, and signed them, there and then.

When the Osteo chap arrived home, he told his wife he'd signed them up with Susie to join The Sparefellows. "Sparefellows, what bird brained idea is this. You are not getting me to show my left nipple and do that funny handshake". "Ha-ha, you are funny", said her husband, "It's only men who have to do that". The chap didn't tell his wife what the ladies have to do!

Later… On a dark, dank, dismal, dreary drizzling Friday evening, we set off for Back dark street. We passed two ladies of the night on two of the street corners, and some "Druggies pushing their wares. ---we spotted the dimly lit doorway, a loud thunder clap made us jump, and a flash of lightening lit up the entrance to the Hall and two ugly gargoyles on guard leapt out of the stonework above. We pushed the creaking old door open and entered an ante room. There were four doors, the ladies and gent's toilets on the left, the Grand Masters room on the right, and in front of us, the doorway to, The Sparefellows Hall. A turn of the door knob didn't open the door, "Was there a secret word or password we needed? "No, the door seemed stuck, a push with the shoulder and the door burst open with a loud noise, as forty or so faces turned and looked to see who the new people were. Surprisingly the hall was brightly lit, it was packed with people sitting four at a table, in two long rows down the hall. Lining the walls of the hall was beautiful oak panelling, that looked as good as when it was installed when the hall was first built one hundred and fifty years ago. It was taken for granted that this hall, the last remaining in the town, would always be here to serve its members and the 250,000 inhabitants of the town. There were pictures on the wall of past members and ladies and gentlemen who had served as Grand Masters even going back to when the hall first opened. Looking around the hall it appeared some of the members had been present on that first inaugural day. Yet…everyone, including the two tables of young people had a warm smile and pleasant words to say as we were introduced. Johnny Silver took us round to meet everyone. A tall gent, a lifelong member, who helped organise meetings and trips, raise money and ring people up to remind members of the forthcoming events. Johnny walked with a bad limp and had an unfortunate nickname, --- mind you it didn't help when he brought his pet parrot and it sat on his shoulder. We met Big Thomas, a Scotsman, a huge monster of a chap. After joining the Sparefellows he had to wait for three months to attend his first social, extending the doorway width and height and hanging the new imposing heavy door fit in very well, even if it tended to stick to the sides of the casing as we had found out. He'd shake your hand and your whole body would shake. He'd speak politely in a deep scots accent for a couple of minutes, sub titles would have been a great benefit in understanding all he said, however you got some idea of his story. The words you could always understand were, "Call me Tom". Out of respect and a little bit of fear everyone obeyed him and called him by the shortened version of Thomas.

Susie was sitting next to her £10 friend Dora, an octogenarian who lives just with her pussy cat. Dora has a beautiful round face with saucer eyes, ears that twitch up and down, a wide mouth with long willowy whiskers on her top lip and chin. You'll always have pleasant conversation with Dora, but beware, if you sit next to her, for dominoes for instance, she tends to intertwine her legs around yours. We next met Joan, she is a lovely genuine, but huge lady. She has an extremely loud voice, tells good jokes to keep members laughing. However, beware, she will soon put people in their place. She gives you a hug and squeezes the life out of you. My son who came with us to our first few socials, got lost in her bosom one night and missed the first two games of the beetle drive!

The socials at Notbowl are simple affairs—usually an invited speaker, followed by beetle drive, dominoes or a quiz, and sometimes a humorous story or two. Then supper with a large variety of hot and cold food. Four games of Bingo follow, with often a line at £4 and the house at £10 whoooo! All the events throughout the year are purely for enjoyment while you are helping worthwhile local charities. You can be initiated in the Sparefellows and take up some office where there will be some payment made to you for your helpful work. Most people like us, don't get so involved but just go to the monthly socials, then choose the trips out or even go on holidays together. If you would like to join The Sparefellows give me a call, I'll introduce you and of course, ----- pick up my £10's.

The Hat

While leaving the beach at 5:30pm, after enjoying the warm sun and the equally refreshing waters, George came across a hat. He had a straw hat he wore on the beach to try to keep the sun off his face, but this was a baseball hat, well cap. It was mid green in colour, with four labels stitched in, all were of small dimensions. On the small round label at the front was pictured a dolphin. Where the hat was gathered at the top a round metal disc, a little rusty, held it all together. George picked the hat up, "I'll be able to wear this in the sun, walking around or sitting near the sea". His wife Mona replied, "No don't, leave it there where you found it half covered with sand, it's dirty and you don't know who's had it on their head". George kept hold of it, gave it a good washing through. Next day at 4pm on the beach. Mona looked round to George who was sitting a little behind and to one side of her, and said, quite annoyingly, "Take that hat off, you look stupid, thin as you are with that little moustache and narrow lips. People will think I'm with my best gay friend, and not my husband". George replied, "I'll keep it on here in the sun, you know my nose has peeled and this hat will keep it in the shade while I'm reading my book, or when we walk up to the top of the beach later". – "You can walk where you want, I won't be by your side unless you put your nice straw hat on; I bought you that from Mat &Co for this holiday." "Yes, and I've worn it for over a week, and now my nose is burned. With this hat, factor 30 and some shade, I'm hoping for a normal looking nose in a few days, before we leave for home". On the last day, when leaving the beach

George placed the green hat under some sand near the top of the beach.

Two days later after a tropical storm had hit the beach, the hat was washed into the sea. A passing boat that had just dropped people off on the isle of Gaybos, passed by, and the lone sailor spotted a green object in the water. He fished the hat out with a hook on the end of a long pole. He shook the hat and placed it on his head. He then headed his boat for Africa.

A man sat on a beach in North Africa, he watched as a round green object slowly came closer on the incoming surf. It washed up in between the man's feet. "Nice one", he said quietly, "Just the job for me today". The man was in his mid-twenties, and had flown to two other countries, and now he was here on a beautiful beach in North Africa. He was a million miles away from his home in Iredale Lancashire.

Two days later a man in his late fifties was driving his high-powered jet-ski just off the same beach where the man from Lancashire had sat. He had anchored his boat, a small, modern yacht, only a few forbidden yards/metres from the shore. Then he drove his machine at top speed only yards from people bathing in the sea, showering them with water, waves and the smell of fuel from the exhaust. He continued in the same vein for hours, sometimes alone on the jet ski, and other times with one of the three crew members from his sleek and elaborate yacht. On one of the journeys on tandem, he cut a turn too sharp and both riders hit the water, with the jet ski floundering to a stop some fifty yards away. There was a roar from bathers and those on the beach who saw it, cheering and clapping, hoping that would put an end to their daily antics. Unfortunately, both riders managed with their life jackets to keep afloat, swim back and climb back on the noisy machine. The driver with a green baseball cap on now. For another two hours the annoying machine ruined a nice peaceful afternoon for those who still remained in the sea or on the shore. Gradually all the people left the beach to the selfish, uncaring and dangerous examples of human life.

The small round label that George and Mona saw on the front of the green hat showed a dolphin turning the other way, as it was in the distance it was shown smaller. The couple had been married now for three years, both were in their late twenties. Mona's family were well off and had given their only daughter all she asked for. George was a "happy go lucky", chap. A painter and decorator by trade, he had lots of good mates and interests. Mona always wanted her own way, and George for a peaceful time, agreed to do her will. Gradually the differences between them, starting off like a small crack, grew to the size of a chasm. The marriage was shaking, and the holiday didn't change a thing. Both George and Mona realised there was no use in going on with the marriage. Within two weeks of the holiday they had mutually agreed to the inevitable and started the divorce proceedings.

The man who dropped off the people at Lesbos, had seen the rectangular label showing a blue and green sea with high surf; it looked nice and colourful! He was on his way back to the North African Coast to collect another 150 or so African people, some who were refugees, and others hoping for a better life in Europe. The man had become very rich, charging £10,000 for the trip per person. Three miles off the coast of Africa, the winds changed, the seas grew rougher, and the torrential rain was mixed with sand from the Sahara Desert. The storm grew worse, waves tossed the boat around, and along with a lightning strike that struck the man in the chest, the boat broke up and capsized. The burnt remains of the man and £200,000 in cash sinking down to Davy Jones's Locker.

The man from Iredale in Lancashire, walking along the Sungier beach on the North African Coast, had picked the hat up and looked at the label on the left side of the hat. A colour picture showing the sea, a beach, and in the distance a volcano showering all the colours of the rainbow upwards. The man returned to his hotel room which overlooked the beach. One hour later he wrapped around his torso a wide belt and fitted it tight to his body. The belt contained pockets of high explosives, sharp nails and ball bearings. He put on his long summer shirt. Then he pulled up his long Bermuda shorts, which had internal pockets stitched in on each outside leg, where he placed two hand guns. He picked up his Kalashnikov rifle, put it in an open shoulder bag, and threw a large beach towel over his shoulder covering the butt of the rifle. He tied his sandals on his feet and put the green hat on his head with the brim of it shadowing his face. He walked out onto the top of the beach. The nearest tourists, mainly English people, were some 75 yards away on sun loungers, under cabanas or umbrellas. The big tourist hotel was situated behind them. The sun was behind the man from Iredale, he went to take the green hat off his head, meaning to put it in his shoulder bag. As the bag was on his right shoulder he lifted the hat with his left hand by the brim, brought it down towards his chest, and the back of the hat where the plastic straps used for tightening the hat caught on something under his shirt. The man still looking straight ahead at his victims, his mind on killing as many as he could, tugged hard on the brim of the hat and triggered the mechanism on his suicide vest. There was a massive explosion and the man was blown to smithereens, small parts of him littering the beach for many yards around where he had stood. The explosion frightened the people 50 yards away from where he had stood, but not a single person was killed or even slightly injured.

The man on the jet ski, with his three comrades on board his yacht, had been high on some of the drugs they were bringing back from Africa to Spain. He now wore the green hat. Just above the hole at the back of the green hat was a label depicting a skull and cross bones, the man smiled at such a fitting picture. They were only a few miles off the Spanish coast with their jet ski and booty on board, when they spotted a boat with sails heading fast towards them. Soon the ship was alongside. The ship had three sails and a flag showing skull and cross bones on it. The "sailors" were of dark skin, pirates from off the African coast. The pirates brandished machine guns and shot the four men. They then raided the small yacht for all that was there, money, drugs, jewellery and some items of clothing. Then they turned the yacht over sinking both the boat and the jet ski.

The hat floated up to the surface as did the four bodies. All were retrieved from the waters in Ramalleb on the Costa Del Sol in Southern Spain. The four bodies, with the clothes they had on, including the green baseball cap were buried in the local cemetery. An inscription on the headstone of the grave tells the story of the men and the green hat. This is why along the Costa Del Sol, from Gibraltar to Malaga you will never see a Spanish person, man or lady, wearing a green hat, and in the whole of that region you will never find a green hat for sale in any tourist or local shop.

The Black Summer of 2020

I am safely housed in deepest rural Lancashire with my family, in our relative's farmhouse home. Looking back, the interruptions to flights in the UK and Europe due to the small Icelandic dusting of ash in April, seem just a minor event. Yet we know it was a prodding from Mother Nature, for us all to look again at how we spend our lives, and what damage daily we do to the environment. Finally, we knew we must do something to help change the destiny of this beautiful planet.

We took little heed of the warning. In June the political parties argued constantly, each trying to protect their own rights and to please their voters, the whole political system was in total disarray. The weather with temperatures in the high 90's for weeks saw racial and religious tensions flare up. Thousands of people were killed in riots and protests. Billions of pounds in criminal damage in damage to houses, shops and public buildings.

The weeks of extreme heat in England was followed by weeks of torrential rain and hell-like horrendous winds and storms, cyclones, earthquakes, and then cataclysmic events;

massive volcanic eruptions, never seen before in this world's history. Iceland was totally evacuated as their land turned into one giant erupting avenging monster of fire and death. Like a giant frog spewing hell onto the earth. The volcanic running lava consuming white hot fire and toxic ash, decimating large parts of cities and towns in the UK. Like plagues of rats leaving the sinking ship, millions of people left the UK for safer havens, never again to return to their cultural homelands. The channel tunnel already flooded, was broken up and completely destroyed.

The day of the full moon in July, with the extra high tides and risen sea levels engulfed and shattered the Thames Barrier. The houses of parliament were flooded, and two days later completely crushed with molten lava. All airports were closed. B.A. and other carriers were no more, as all their planes were scattered debris or burnt out wrecks.

It was now September, I crossed the road last week from our new home. It was midday, but the air was still dark. We had not seen the full sun since those barmy early June days. I posted my new voting paper as a gentle breeze pervaded the atmosphere. As I turned for home, more and more light came through the dense bleakness and soon all was clear.

The iridescent and happy blue sky, the glowing sun reaching its arms of rays down to the glorious magnificent English countryside. The villages, houses and farms below, and the lucky inhabitants inside were safe, and able to carry on in their daily lives. We had learned our lessons; the past months had changed our whole outlook on life. We knew now our lives had to be lived in line with nature. It was a life that would be simpler, rewarding and, most of all, totally peaceful.

Summer Sunday Trip

The day in Summer in England when we all hope to enjoy a warm sunny Sunday. The weather forecast was for rain to arrive late afternoon, great we'll be on our way back then. We let, rather foolishly, our ten-year-old son Tom, because he too likes Lytham St. Anne's choose our trip. "Black Pool", he joyously yelled, and he reeled off all the two for ones or 20% off; Madam Tussauds, The Tower, Pleasure Beach, and the eating places on his I Phone.

We set off from home at Ten am, with just a drip drop on the windscreen. By the time we got to Chorley on the M61 it was normal English rain. On to the M6 and it was monsoonal, with the wish wash of the wipers unable to cope, and all vehicles staying in lane at a steady thirty miles per hour, unusual all drivers behaving well.

A stress-free run, and entered Wilko's car park in good time, minutes before eleven am. With our raincoats on and three umbrellas' in use, we journeyed to the Winter Gardens, where we were entertained by groups of various kinds of dancing troupes, all trying their best to win the £20,000 first prize. We left there and went into the Tower, had a look around and then sat and watched couples doing the Viennese waltz, rumba and quickstep. As the magic sounds of the Wurlitzer organ filled the ballroom, a glimmer of sunlight lit up the whole room for a magic minute. We walked out of the Tower, crossed the new tram lines onto the comedy carpet, as the rain was easing, and spent half an hour reading some of the comedy legends famous lines. We then crossed the road and tram lines and had a bite to eat in Coral Island, £15 was the first money we'd spent so far!

Being a bank holiday Blackpool was Packed. We crossed again over to the promenade and towards the impressive steps that lead down to the beach. At that moment when we caught sight of the sea, some fifty yards from the beach, a warming breeze blew gently onto our faces, the three of us turned around at the same moment, as though synchronised, and saw tens of thousands of smiles appearing on the happy faces of the visiting throng. Simultaneously spirits were lifted, which had the effect of a fast motion film pushing back the dark clouds, which disappeared from view. The day was transformed from cold and dark as hell, to a warm and sunny heaven.

There were angels and cherubs riding on the sun's rays. People were singing and dancing on the Golden Mile, some folks not even needing a "Kiss Me Quick" hat or t-shirt. On the prom even "straight" couples were hugging and kissing. As we walked on Central Pier, the sea below was of a translucent turquoise. There were mermaids near the lapping of the warm waves edge onto the beach, and scores of happy dolphins leaping joyously out of the water. Fishermen on the end of the pier were landing shoals of fish, each fish with a smile on its face, as the fishermen returned their capture to their home in the sea.

We finished the day off in Bond Street Chippy; cod, chips and peas for two, and haddock chips and peas for me, all with bread and real butter, rounded off with a cup of tea. It seemed we'd never enjoyed a meal so much. It clearly was the best day out ever!

Looking up, Falling Down

At the beginning of this month, my wife and I were dining out with my bestest two mates from school and through our teenage years into our twenties. Chris and Mick who were, of course, accompanied by their wives Diane and Posh Gill.

The boys were laughing and joking, you see I'm a little older than them. "Oh, it's your big birthday next week John". And on a more serious note, "I hope you've made a will, have you made your own funeral arrangements yet?"

My big birthday, you get one every ten years with a zero at the end. It came and went yet was very enjoyable.

The next day I was working on a magnificent spreading chestnut tree; thinning the dead, diseased, and dangerous branches. I'd finished the work and had just started my descent, when the branch that I was anchored to broke, and I fell some 50 feet. A journey that seem to last a lifetime; It wasn't frightening, like when I skied down an uneven wet slate roof, on a foggy day one February. I hit the wooden ladder, bent the irons back and it catapulted me high up into the air, and I landed a way off on a brick pillar and smashed my right leg. No this wasn't frightening, it was peaceful with beautiful pictures of my past life. Someone must have lifted me up, because I looked down and saw myself, well my body on the ground. The lady of the house, where the tree stood came out and screamed, "God Almighty Save Him", and then looking closer exclaimed, "He's dead". Her diagnosis was right, they buried me just an hour ago.

Here I am now with friends and relatives in Heaven, in another dimension, looking down, checking on how the buffet is going after my burial. My friend Chris talking about those great days of playing football for the school and the teams later on, and all the great times together. "Yeah", said Mick, "Oh he was such a nervous boy, when asked a question in class he'd er-err, um- er-er and not be able to answer". "and he'd believe anything you said, he was as green as grass". "Yep", said Chris, "Now he's pushing up the grass, and the daisies!". "Remember the school trip to London. We told him the best-looking girl in the school wanted to go out with him". "Yeah, and he left us and sat next to her on the coach and walked everywhere she went". "Yep, and when the teachers dragged us to the London Palladium to see the Sammy Davis Junior Show, he sat next to her and bought her toffee and ice-cream. She was a beautiful girl, a funny looking skinny kid with big buck teeth had NO CHANCE".

"John and spotty, cross-eyed, dumpy, tree trunk legged Cheryl were together for two years, engaged for six months." "Yeah, I went with him for his first pair of glasses to Specsavers, the day before he broke off their engagement". After that he moved away to Notlob, away from the old antique to a new model. The new model thought John had loads of money, and John thought Susan was minted. Piteeee, here I'll get you another pint".

Diane and Gill were talking together over their white wines. "He would have survived the fall, if he'd had some meat on his bones, poor chap he was as thin as a rake".-His wife's a vegetarian you know, they drink that decapitated tea and eat Stella McCartney sausages"---"They did that cross legged stuff"—"Oh you mean Quorn chicken legs, we get them, used to be cheap till yon runner started advertising them". ---"No, that meditation where they do that humming". — "Om Om you mean. Pity he didn't do that flying technique, he wouldn't have needed the climbing rope, he could have just flown on to the branches like a bird". – "Yeah with his chicken legs he'd look like a stork with his hat and visor over its beak, and a chainsaw in its wing". — "He had a big one". ---"I never knew you went out with him, did you?"— "No, no, I mean he had a big beak, a big conk". – "You did say conk, didn't you?" ---"Yes Conk". – "Probably why he didn't get married till he was 38". – "Somebody, well Sandra from Stacksteads, told me he had other tendencies." "I wondered why he walked funny".—"No not tendencies, I mean she said he batted for the other side".---"Well I never".—"Yes indeed".---"I knew he played football and Brian their goalie became a famous cricketer for Lancashire, but I never knew he played cricket for Yorkshire".

Even I started to laugh, and then I was being shaken. Was it time to move on from this heaven, looking down on my funeral in the company of my dear family and friends? No, it was my wife shaking me awake, "You keep waking me up with your laughing out loud, what were you dreaming of?" I replied, "Oh, just about when we were with Chris, Mick, Diane and Posh last week". ---"Well you've had a lovely birthday today, get back to sleep or you'll be late tomorrow at Mrs. Ecclescakes. You've got to trim her beautiful spreading chestnut tree, God Bless."

"Err - God Bless!".

The Story of Jack and Jill

There was a man called Jack, who lived at the bottom of the hill in Notlob, (in Darcy Lever, with the "Village People"). He had a small business, a devoted wife Jill, and three beautiful happy children.

Now age 40, his friends were telling him," you're over the hill now Jack, it's all downhill for you now". Well he had a couple of grey hairs, a few worry lines, and was finding it harder to get out of bed in the mornings, due to increasing aches and pains. You see Jack had worked increasingly hard for the last twenty-five years, and he knew he had to relax more, enjoy life, and as he read in The News of The World: Live healthily.........FOR EVERMORE!

Jack went out and bought all the wonder creams and body lotions you see advertised on the television, and many very expensive ones off the internet, even though many of the ingredients were not shown on the labels. He applied the face creams three times daily, in an effort to see himself in the mirror, with the same youthful face that he had when he was twenty-one years of age. Whenever he could get in the bathroom, or in the bedroom, he would strip off his clothes, and liberally cover his body from foot to head, in body lotions, creams or oils. One day his wife Jill caught him:

thinking this was a new preparation for them to have a cuddle together, her eyes lit up, her face became flushed, she felt a quivering throughout her body, and advanced towards Jack, throwing off her dressing gown, her arms outstretched, her lips pouting like fresh figs she enfolded her husband in her arms, her body pressed next to his, she squeezed her arms together......... and due to the abundance of oil on Jack's body he slid out of her grasp like a wet bar of soap, shot head first over Jill's shoulder and banged his head on the laminate flooring.

The ambulance crew weren't too impressed, though the day before they'd rescued a lady with her big toe stuck up into her bathroom tap, no problem for them once they pulled her husband out of the bath, who said he had come to help her. After four hours in A and E Jack was cleared to go home, neither Jack or Jill who drove him home were so happy. However, lessons were learned, and Jack reluctantly stopped the lathering on of oils. He still believed he could turn back the clock and searched for the answer to regain his lost looks and athleticism.

On his way home from work one day, Jack saw a notice in the window of a private clinic, it promised "Mind and Body Rejuvenation". Jack took down the 'phone number and booked an appointment.

Firstly, Jack had a consultation with a Doctor Quackman, who prescribed ghastly, ooh nasty medicines to ingest. This was followed by long, hot and laborious oil massages, this by two male therapists in tandem. These massages were to rid the organs and tissues of impurities. Next, he was laid in a wooden sweat box, with heat underneath, and just his head sticking out, till he was "cooked", sweat draining from every pore and his skin the colour of beetroot. This he was told would get the debris draining into his digestive tract. A shattered and drained Jack was helped into a pure white sheeted bed, and a cover thrown over him. Jack was just starting to dose off, when the door opened, and the white coated therapist walked in carrying a bag with some brown liquid in it which had a small pipe attached. He asked Jack to turn on his side with one leg bent a little, smeared his bottom with something, told him of the procedure, and carried on with the warm oil and herb enema. Jack was told this was to clear his system of poisonous toxic wastes. The problem was Jack had booked for five days treatment, not only did he feel his body had been cleared out, but a big chunk of his bank balance had been cleared out too.

Instead of seeing more of his wife Jill and his three beautiful teenage children, Jack always seemed to be busy elsewhere. This time he was off to India. "I'm doing it for you darling and the kids; I'll be able to look after you much better when I return".

Jack stayed for three months in India, the entire time spent in a wooden box. All his hair fell out, along with his teeth, and he now weighed seven stone, down from a healthy looking eleven stone. After six months recovering at home Jack's weight was up to nine and a half stone, his teeth were in, and his hair was back, apart from on his head where once had adorned beautiful black wavy hair.

Jack stayed at home for the next two years, saving to go to Russia, or Central Asia. While his wife and three beautiful children were enjoying holidays together, Jack could be found having "Health Treatments" at the local hose pipe clinic, usually enduring the special Push- Flush- and Gush……

Jack then wearily jetted off to the former Russian state of Staniknockitov, to have the famous; Memory Intelligence Consciousness Kryptonite, treatment, with the renowned professor Iva Slataloose. This is where special electric ores, yes ores, are placed on the body and head to clear the body and brain of past impressions.

Jack recovered from having the past impressions, or Memory Intelligence Consciousness Krytonite, M.I.C.K., mick taken out of him, which took three months and the last of his money, in a spa by the black sea.

Was Jack any better after all the treatments, and money, he had gone through? ------He looked at himself in the full-length mirror. He looked at his feet, then slowly up his legs, above his knees, "ooh". He then looked at his body, his abdomen, his chest, "oohooh". He leaned his head forward and looked at his head and face, his eyes and mouth now wide open. And finally looked between the top of his legs and his abdomen, "ooooooo", and threw both his hands to cover that special area; well it was just in case anyone came in the room and found him naked. ------- Jack's body was slender and athletic, there were no veins showing or age spots. His hair was back, it was glossy black, wavy-lustrous-beautiful. His teeth were perfect, and there wasn't a wrinkle in sight. He was strong and flexible, and could do the times crossword, or the daily sport Sudoku in two minutes. He looked just twenty-two years of age and had an I.Q. of one hundred and ninety…. two!

This handsome and attractive twenty-two-year-old went for the plane back to Manchester. Before he arrived back home, he'd noticed how young ladies had stared at him admiringly; their mouths wide open, tongues fallen out, dripping with want, and saliva! But Jack had no want, he'd no desire for any younger partner. His mind was pure, and he only wanted? Yes, you know what he wanted, he only wanted to be back with his lovely wife Jill, and his three wonderful, beautiful children.

Jack tried his key in the door of his home, 153 Acacia street. He widdled the key in and out, but the key could not turn the lock. So, Jack knocked hard on the wooden front door. An Indian gentleman opened the door; he wore a brightly coloured feathered headdress, that reached above his head and sloped right down to the level of the backs of his knees. He had stripes of paint on both cheeks, chin and across his forehead, he carried a tomahawk in his right hand which he raised to head height: "Hello sir, what do you want?" he asked. Jack took a step back, and replied, "I err, err... live here". The Indian gentleman said, "OH sir, I bought this house off your wife, here is the letter she asked me to give you".

Jack took the letter and crossed the road to the park. It was a drizzly dreary, dark, dank, dismal, depressing, disappointing kind of day. Jack sat down on a vandalised wet wooden bench. He opened the letter and started to read.

It was a good job it was in indelible ink, it was that drizzle that wets you through.

Jack's wife Jill had left him and was now living at the top of the hill in the posh part of town - at the top of Markland Hill. She was with a person who everyone looked up to and admired greatly, for the wonderful work he, (yes, it is a man), had done over many years in that town. His three beautiful, happy AND intelligent children, were in the best universities that money could buy.

His wife Jill was deeply in love with the vicar, who was cross-eyed, had a face like the back of a rhinoceros, was hump backed, had three bellies' and bow legs that you could drive a double decker bus through. But at last Jill had found her true love, her soul mate.

And Jack; all what he loved, besides himself, had been taken away. He had no family ......no friends...he had no desire, nothing. He was a forty-five-year-old man in a twenty-two-year-old body. Jack died with misgivings, regret and deep sadness twelve months later...in a dirty, damp, rotten, stinking, rat infested, hovel of a shed, on the banks of the river Croal.

The moral of this story is, as Jill knows," Beauty IS only skin deep". Or as Jack now knows, "Beauty is six feet deep".

A Day at The Beach

It was August school holidays and the temperature was a constant 90 degrees during the day. That is 90 degrees in or out of the waters on Florida's Gulf Coast. The Aquamarine sea lazily splashed its gentle surf onto the pristine white flour, that carpeted the immaculate beach. Each morning we spent an hour on the beach, and usually an hour or two late afternoons. Each time I'd swim a short distance out to the sandbank, where you could walk with the waters only reaching up to your shorts; …or in my case, being a short...person, above my shorts.

It was a cloudless, clear blue Thursday morning. I put my Ken Follet paperback down, rose from my little beach chair, said, "See you in a few minutes", to my wife Sylvia. Tightened the string on my jazzy blue and white swim shorts and walked the few yards to the edge of the sea.

It was very quiet on the beach, just a few people enjoying the peace and quiet. I passed by various large wading birds with pink bills and matching pink feet, half a dozen egrets, and lots of miniature birds who ran quick with their little legs from the wet sand into the water and back.

Nobody noticed as I waded into the warm water, the iridescent wet reaching up to my waist, before I slowly stretched forward with my arms, bent my body and plunged headlong into the inviting sea. I swam leisurely the small distance to the sandbank, scattering shoals of small fish. And what was unusual, the same fish kept coming back in front of me, again and again. I walked fifty yards north on the sandbank and looked up about another one hundred yards, to see a crowd of people pointing from the beach out to sea. It was usual early mornings to see Dolphins swimming north, some days you'd see just a couple, other days as many as ten or twelve diving in and out of the waters as they sped on their joyous course. It was now four in the afternoon; the Dolphins must be on their way back south. The people on the beach were getting more and more excited, shouting and waving. All the folk who had been anywhere near them in the water, were now back on the beach. The ever-gathering crowd were walking steadily down the beach in my direction, still pointing out a little distance in the sea. Two men left the group and ran in my direction, waving and gesturing……. To get out of the sea. I looked to see a large dorsal fin sleekly gliding through the water about seventy yards away from me. It was on the inside of the sandbank where I stood in some four feet of water… It was clear now… It was a shark. I thought about swimming to the shore, but any movement or splashing in the water, let alone my fear producing bodily fluids, would arouse the shark, and its speed would mean…I would be caught!....I decided, as my legs shook in unison, to stay as still as I could, and hoped and prayed it would pass me by.

Only thirty yards away now, and I could make out a vague outline of its body. For a moment I thought it might be a whale, it was massive, it was frighteningly huge. Barely twenty yards away now; there was a splinter of blue light. Its head broke out of the sea turning to the right, sending huge torrents of water ten feet high and across, drenching and knocking me sideways for a second. I stood there cold and trembling in fear, seeing the big white head, menacing eyes, and its cavernous mouth open showing the top and bottom of a curtain of white razor-sharp teeth. Then the great whites head touched down on the water, raised up its head its mouth now closed, and shook violently from side to side, pulling-----tearing---ripping open its meal/prey, sending globules of blood into the air and torrents of red into the purple sea. Splattered with blood and bits of flesh I watched the beasts dorsal fin and then its tail fin pass me by on its way south. No doubt quietly satisfied, replete with parts of the flesh of that big tarpon fish in its belly.

I stood for a while, tears rolling down my face. Then I slowly swam back to shore, thanking that fish for being alongside of me, at the moment the great white shark struck, ----And thanking God for saving my life.

Brian and the Devil Dog's Dumplings

Brian had always been alright with dogs. As a young child living on a farm he loved Lad and Lassie the two Border Collies. Both dogs had a line of white fur over their friendly faces. The two dogs would follow Brian anywhere, and in any seasonal weather, even though deep snow around their hillside farm.

When Brian was nine years of age the family moved from the farm, this was due to two bad winters, when the farm was locked in with snow as high as the upstairs windows of the farmhouse.

Living now in a terraced house was no good for a dog with everyone out at work, yet after a couple of years a new Lassie came to the household. The new member of the house was a playful border collie puppy. Lassie wasn't very obedient if you were taking her for a walk through the fields. The instinct was there - Lassie would get down in the familiar crouching position, weighing up the sheep in the field, and then she was off chasing and rounding them up. After a while, anywhere near animals Lassie had to be on the lead. It was somewhat a mystery when Lassie "vanished". She was always allowed off the lead around the street where they lived, next thing she was gone, never to be seen again. Had she been run over by a vehicle and killed, a fatality of road traffic? That was unlikely, as no one had heard of a dog being hit on the road. If Lassie was dead, it was most likely caused by a farmer with his six-bore rifle. Perhaps a farmer had caught Lassie and took him to a farm in another area to train as a sheep dog, this explanation was given to the younger children, Lassie was now happy and content doing what she liked doing best.

Brian's father Dick, bought his youngest daughter June a yellow Labrador pup. The daughter loved the puppy, but with everyone out of the house all day it wasn't the best for the puppies came to the rescue, when he read in the local newspaper of a small girl age eight who's pet Labrador of one year had ran out of the front door and was run over and killed by a passing police car. Dick rang the 'phone number in the paper. The little girl and her family were so grateful to take the Labrador puppy. A good news story, following up from the little girl who lost her puppy, was in the newspaper along with a photograph of the puppy, the little girl and her family, plus Dick and June.

Brian didn't have much to do with any dog's after the Labrador, no more entered their home. Years later Brian had married and was living with his wife Gloria and their two children. Two Sundays out of the month Brian worked as a volunteer ranger at South West Pennines Stumbles Centre. The main area Brian worked and patrolled was around the three reservoirs. While out doing various work, one of the duties was to give dog owners, "Poopascoops", to make it easy for them to pick their dog's excrement up. It was amazing just how many dog owners thought it was alright to let their pets poo on the paths, just off the paths, or farther off on grass or in bushes, and then, leave the foul mess there. However, after a friendly chat explaining the dangers of the problem, they all, without exception took the new scoops and promised in future to pick the dada up. It was easier to do with the poopascoop, shovel it and cover it with the bag attached, no problem. The footpaths and verges around the reservoirs did improve, walkers now not having to keep their eyes down to the ground, but able to look around at all the beautiful countryside, wildlife and birdlife.

One day Brian set off in the car to get some business cards printed at a friend's shop. As he was leaving the shop his friend accompanied him to the shop door and chatted for a while. Brian then walked down a block to where his car was parked. As he drove off he thought there was something under his foot, but he didn't take any notice of it. Within one minute there was an awful stink in the car. The dog poo stuck in the grooves in the soles of his new shoes was sending out the horrible stench that was pervading the car. Brian wound all the windows down but when he had to stop at traffic lights he was close to passing out. He was close to keeling over from the pong when he arrived home. He dived out of the car, threw the car floor mat out and threw his shoes at the side of it. Brian had a cool drink and then filled a bucket with soap, disinfectant and hot water, he then went and cleaned the mess up.

While washing away the mess Brain was rather annoyed shouting loudly "DOG POO, EXCREMENT, DUNG, FAECES, STOOL, DEJECTIONS, HORRIBLE UNSIGHTLY SMELLY STUFF, ALL THIS ON MY SHOES AND IN THE CAR!" No passers-by stopped but carried on hurriedly due to the tone of Brian's voice. Brian said aloud, "There must be a link between dog's and their dogged owners". He then looked up, past the parked car to the two little brick pillars on each side of the drive, and sure enough there was a tidy heap deposited by a large dog next to the pillar on the right. Brian went inside for another bucket of disinfected water, a poopascoop and a long-handled brush. This pillar event was happening four or five times a week. Soapy water, bleach, even growing nettles near the pillar didn't deter the dogs or their owners who never picked their mess up. Next to the left-hand pillar there was a concrete street lamp post with a sign some ten feet, (3meters), from the ground. This was put there by Notbowl Metro Council stating, 2This is a designated area", and a fine up to £1,000 for dog fouling. Brian understood, especially at ten feet high that the dogs may not be able to see it, let alone read it. The dog owners, Brian was incensed with their attitude, as well as frustrated and sick of clearing their mess. He decided to try to catch one of them.

He tried to take photos of them, but never got a convincing shot, though he had pictures of before, during and after the dog's visit. Brian next placed a tape recorder at the base and back of the pillar on the right. He planned to run down the path, confront the dog owner about the newly dropped mess, and if there was any trouble he'd make a citizen's arrest, phone the police and see the person in court. The only thing on the recorder was Brian's footsteps racing to the incident. While recovering in hospital from a punch that the six-foot, fifteen stone selfish moron threw at him, Brian vowed to do everything in his power to stop this health and safety hazard. He wrote to the Prime Minister, the Minister for health and local M.P.'s; all of them......did nothing! He asked local councillors, and after many months they helped Brian and hundreds of others in the same position to form a group. The C.A.C.S, Campaign Against Canine Stools.

At the inaugural meeting of CACS the Notbowl Mayor, herself a victim of the dreaded mess, asked everyone to put it on their social media outlets, Facebook, twitter and others. We all wore large badges with CACS in large letters. We had a CACS guide book containing all the steps to take to approach the general public, and how to deal with any occurrence of malignant dropping of the said matter. The Lady Mayor in her most authoritative beaming voice declared, "Be Vigilant, Be Together". To this day those four words survive as CACS motto, and when two members meet, both parties say this to each other, then the CACS hug, the head to shoulder movements to each shoulder, the elbow grip with the left hand while the right-hand rests on the others left shoulder, all done in four seconds flat. Lately some members had started to say the four letters of CACS aloud to the four movements. Brian preferred the quieter, simple and natural way. He said the speaking aloud of CACS damaged the purity and innocence of the meeting of two people with the same desire; to rid the world of the nuisance, and waste of man's valuable time.

The Lady Mayor asked us always to wear our badge, carry extra poopascoops and ask dog owners to start to collect their dog's posher mention as it was Winter time, the poo would help to keep their hands warm while walking their passive they won't pick it up, she remarked, Report Them. Somehow anyhow we have to cure and cleanse Notbowl of this danger to society….She was getting more animated by the minute. THESE NASTY DOG OWNERS, WHO ARE HEADSTONG, INFLEXIBLE, INTRACTABLE, MULISH, OBSTINATE, STUBBORN, UNYIELDING,

WILFUL, MOROSE, SOUR, SULLEN AND SURLY, have to be shown it is wrong to let their dogs foul public or private places and not to clean it up. It is DIRTY, FOUL, SMELLY, DANGEROUS AND POSSIBLY FATAL TO HEALTH. Members of CACS we will cure Notbowl of the mess and go on to make all of Britain a cleaner and safer place to live and walk. In the next twelve months seven dog owners were fined in Notbowl, none of them the full £1,000. Gradually as another twelve months went by no more fines were given out and the scourge returned, poo by the pillars, soft, hard, big or little drops, smeared pavements and grass verges. The incidents of people, including many children, being hospitalised from Toxocariasis grew. Hospitals couldn't cope with cases of Colitis, E-Coli, Dysentery, Typhoid, undiagnosed Rashes, fits, cramps, fever, diarrhoea, headaches and even Cholera and Kidney disorders. Most parts of the body were at risk, eye problems sometimes leading to blindness, lung, heart, neurological and various organ ailments. Twenty-three faecal colitorum bacteria, whip, hook, round and tape worms. Parvo, Corona, Giardiasis, Salmonellosis, Campylobuteriosis and Crytosporidiosis, all possible causes of the hospitals being overcrowded, yet no manager, councillor or M.P. mentioned the link to dogs. Even cases of

Even cases of roundworm and others in people and animals, who had no pets and had not been near any, wasn't blamed on dog poo. Yet on their lawns or grass years before there were deposits of dog's dung, and the eggs of roundworm and others had lingered in the soil till the innocent person or pet had walked on that area. All this was costing the country a fortune, not only health-wise, but tourism hit an all-time low. No tourist wanted to go to a country where you were fenced off from going anywhere near the sea, plus the risk of an accident or illness and they would have little chance of seeing a doctor or getting hospital treatment. The Prime Minister and most M.P.'s did not dare to come out and say it was all down to most families in the UK having a dog and 90% of them leaving mess where their pet stopped, be it village, town, country or seaside, oh no, the MP's might lose votes!

Emigration from the UK to many parts of the world was increasing at an unprecedented rate as the months went by. The opposite was happening with dog's. Illegal dogs imported via the internet or smuggled in to the British Isles from various countries, never having any vaccinations or health checks was rife. Alabama Foot Rot cases during the winter months escalated, as did Shuttleworth's Bottom Disease during the summer months.

It looked like the British Isles would never recover from the damage to the environment caused by The Devil Dog's Dumplings.

It was a sad place for Brian and the few who knew the truth. Even a few dog owners were disturbed at the outlook, which was already very grim. It looked like the British Isles were doomed……….AND THEN, when it seemed it was impossible for this once green and pleasant land to disintegrate further, a miracle started slowly to come into place. Had Mother Nature seen enough? had she looked at all the different breeds of dogs, so distant from the wolf?

Breeders of small dogs, toy dogs, had noticed their dog's litters getting smaller, the pups who were born where getting weaker.

Owners of toy dogs were constantly seeing their pets drop out of their handbags or find them too poorly to move suffering from a variety of illnesses affecting Gastric, Kidney, Heart, Fungal Diseases and Cancer. Soon most toy breeds were wiped out, Chihuahua, Pomeranian, Pugs, Shih Tzu, Pekinese, French Bulldog and others. Last of them to go was the Yorkshire Terier. The only surviving Toy Dog was the Bichen Frise.

The next to go were the hybrid dogs; Cockapoo, Cavapoo, Chavachon, Labradoodle and Sprocker. The dogs that survived the best were Shiva Inus, Belgian Malinors, Baseujis, Australian Cattle Dog, Bichen Frise, limited Poodle and Greyhounds, Beagles, English Springer Spaniels and Border Collies. German Shepherd Dogs with their joint, gastric, lupus, pancreatic, degenerative myelopathy stood no chance of surviving when they caught the other diseases.

The dog population in the UK had grown from 10 million to 14 million during the four bad years. Over the last few years the dog population had been decimated to just half of the 2017 numbers at 5 Million. It seemed each night on the TV there were programmes about the scourge. Panorama revealing at last the truth about the whole episode. Shortly after a high licence fee for owners, (some less well-off elderly people and the blind were exempted), was brought in by the Government. Fines for fouling in public places were trebled, and for a second offence it was jail for the offending dog owner. No one could now own a dog bought off the internet, in fact those selling dogs on the web were hunted down and jailed or worse. CACS became a registered charity with the Queen and Prime Minister as patrons. The whole country prospered as all the beaches around the British Isles flew the Green Flag and the seas had high stocks of healthy fish, sea creatures and bird life. Tourists flocked in from abroad to holiday in the once more green and fragrant land.

Brian and Gloria's two children were both married now, with children of their own. Before their retirement Brian and Gloria had said they would have a border collie puppy. However, upon them both retiring they found their days were filled with other things; being with and helping family and friends, having a social life and continuing to have short breaks around the British Isles, and now a month abroad in the sun. Did they deserve to enjoy their retirement so much? They had worked hard in their jobs, and for many years put lots of their "spare time", and effort into their vocation, their passion of pursuing the goal of CACS. Some might say leaving it all to others, having no contact with CACS is just selfish! None of this bothered Brian or Gloria, it never entered their heads. They never even thought of their monthly subscriptions to, "Dogs for the Blind" or C.A.C.S. They'd led full and useful lives up to retirement, and now, though in a different way, their lives were filled with good and enjoyable works, without any stress, giving them happy and fulfilled days for the rest of their lives.

The Kid With The Iron Fists

There was a kid called Ken. Before his birth in February 1949 it looked like he'd be still born, lifeless, and his mother would die too. Mother was ill in bed and would not go into hospital, even though Doctor O'Shaunessy insisted she must. The kid's father Ken rang for an ambulance, and in due time the baby was born, and mother survived. Mother was still poorly for the next twelve months. Four years later mother gave birth to her last child, a girl who they named Mary. Mary had six sisters and just the one brother Ken.

As Ken started to grow it looked like he'd always be just a thin scraggy lad. It didn't help the kid, when he was six years old he climbed up an old sycamore tree in the park and the branch he sat on broke. It sent Ken careering to the ground, where he hit his head, broke his collar bone, and caused excessive trauma to his spine. Young Ken was taken to hospital, his arm and leg bandaged and sent home. The fact that he was helped into the hospital by the ambulance staff in a wheelchair, waited an hour in a corridor and could hardly stand on his feet, didn't seem to matter. The hospital was too busy in February with an influenza outbreak.

Ken's father got a job at Dolland's pie factory in Rexandon, putting the lids on meat and tater pies. The family of ten moved up to Rexandon, to live in a four-bedroom terraced house. Ken's wife Shelley got a job in Dapiham, filling jars at the treacle mine.

Young Ken, who had done a year at his former school in the little village of Ramsvalley, now had to start afresh at St. Dongoats, four miles away in Basterden. His first morning at St. Dongoats was eventful. Five, Six and seven-year olds shouting abuse and telling him, in more adult language, to get back to Ramsvalley.

Then a lad in the class above Ken started to pull at Ken's new uniform, first his jumper then his short pants. Ken asked the lad to stop but, but when the lad got a handful of soil and started to put it down the front of Ken's pants, Ken said, "STOP". "Stop or what you weakling?" Ken let the lad stand back, showing off in front of all the kids watching, and then, with all that had built up inside him, delivered a straight right jab to the left side of the bully's face. The lad keeled over from the punch and fell to the floor. He saw stars from another universe and lay dazed for the next few minutes. Ken asked if he was alright, "Yes2, and then got in line to enter the classroom. Ken and his assailant Russell were sent to the headmaster; a nice quiet retiring gentleman with a soft tone to his voice. Head gave them both "four" strokes of the cane on the hands. Then he gave Ken two more for the condition of his uniform. At home when Mum and dad returned from work, Ken told them the full story. He received a smacking on the bottom and legs from mother, and a loud harsh telling off from his father, the latter from father hurting him the most.

Two years later the bottom fell out of the pie business at Rexandon. Dad Ken was picking up bits of work but, when the treacle mine dried up the family moved back to Ramsvalley. This time the family were housed in a council house on the then notorious Peelsworth estate. Ken returned to St. Joepecks and all Martyrs, or all tomatoes as the kid's called it. No one took any notice of him, until he went to hang his coat on a hook in the cloakroom. A bunch of lad's followed by some girls crowded around him. One lad, who was well named, Dick, pulled Ken's coat off him and threw it on the floor. "That's my hook you little swine." Ken bent down to pick it up and Dick kicked Ken up the backside, which sent Ken falling onto his coat. There was loud laughing from the crowd. "Get up you buck toothed ugly little pig". Ken got to his feet, "Where can I hang my coat". "Give it to me", Dick said, as he grabbed the coat, I'll put it on the school railings outside, now that it's pouring down". Ken grabbed the end of his coat and pulled it back to him, along with Dick on the other end of his coat. "Please let it go", Ken asked. Dick answered, "Or else what, you wimp?" Ken had grown impatient, the time to talk was over, in a flash he dropped his right hand to his side, bent it back and swung the arm with such velocity turning the fist from an upright position to one of a straight bunch of fives,, and it collided onto the middle of Dick's face, bursting open his nose and sending him reeling backwards, and falling on his bottom on the bench below the coat hangers. The crowd fled. Soon after two teachers arrived on the scene and cleaned Dick up. Mrs. Black took Ken into her classroom, and gave him, "six of the best", with her leather strap on the kid's backside. After that Ken was sent to the headmaster, a stern looking man in his fifties, who didn't stand for any messing. Instead of the caning, Mr. Radley sat Ken down and gently talked to him about the damage that fighting can cause to the brain and body. Ken thanked Mr. Radley, and went back to Mrs. Black's class, where she put him in a corner with a white cap that came together in a point about a foot above Ken's head, t had a large capital D in black on the front. It was a relief for Ken to leave Mrs. Black after two years in her class. He'd seemed a normal kid before that class, now he'd become uneasy with all the fear that had been put in him.

Ken's move up to Secondary school looked like a good move. He was ribbed for his accent, a broader Lancashire, but met good mates and got respect for his athletic and football skills. Ken loved his football, he focused on it night and day, which at first had a detrimental effect on his school work. On the surface Ken appeared now like any other kid starting secondary school. He was a little apprehensive at first, then he got into the swing of it. He was back chatting to anyone about anything, like he used to be a few years ago, only now he was told off on more occasions. His "mates" got their friend, the innocent and trusting Ken into a few scraps. In assembly beckoning Ken to turn around in line, and then keeping him talking, as the headmaster, who was raised up on the stage, spotted Ken and shouted, "You lad, to my office immediately after assembly. Four strokes of the cane on the hand followed. One day a tough stout streetwise lad mickey, who was in the year above Ken's first year was bullying kids from Ken's year, pushing, pulling and hitting them, and shouting he'd beat them up. Ken's," mates", had a word with Mickey, then they said to Ken, "Mickey wants to talk to you, to ask you something". Ken refused to go to Mickey but, after being assured it was, "nothing much, he just wants to ask you something". Ken looked down towards the bottom of the hard-surfaced school yard. Mickey saw Ken, and the two of them started to walk towards each other, like two gunslingers up the dusty main street of a small western town. A crowd of lads followed a few yards behind each contestant. They met, "What do you want Mickey?", Mickey replied, "You've said if I don't stop pushing other kids you'd fight me". "No, I did not", Ken said. The crowd behind Mickey urged him on, "Give the kid a clout Mickey", "Send him back to class with a black eye", "Bust his nose". Mickey like an angry wrestler bent low, opened his arms, and like a crouching tiger went for Ken. Ken had hoped for more of a boxing match, he had to step to one side and threw a left jab followed by a right, both shots glanced the sides of Mickey's face and threw him off balance. Ken moved in, but mickey threw himself under Ken's arms and grabbed Ken around the waist pulling both of them onto the tarmac. The two of them pulling pushing and rolling over. Mickey got on top of ken, Ken looked up and could just see a small space where the blue of the sky showed. Some 400 or so boys had crowded in so close, Ken had a job to get his breath, and the noise from the crowd was deafening. Ken had to get to his feet, with all his strength he pulled Mickey over, yet Mickey was tough and both lads were holding each over and rolling around. Ken was trying to get released from Mickey's grip, and mickey was trying to get a stranglehold on Ken. Dring-aling-aling, riiiing, riiiing, the school bell rang, dinner break was over, time to assemble in line with your class. The crowd dispersed rapidly, quick as rats from a swollen flooded river. Ken and Mickey got to their feet, both shaking from their exertions. Both lads looked each other in the eye, Mickey held out his hand, Ken surprised, stretched his right hand out and the waring two made peace with a short handshake, then both of them ran to join their assembled class. Ken walked into school feeling a bit emotional, partly from the fight but, also realising that beneath Mickey's tough exterior there existed a kid who deep down had compassion and respect. The fight had taught Ken a great deal, he realised the 900 kids at the school all had similar feelings as himself, and from now on he'd try not to judge other kids, or, even grown-ups. Mickey too seemed a changed kid, he joined in with other kids in class and playing in the school yard. He was happier and the smiles on his face, along with the interaction with others was a triumph, for him, kids and teachers alike. Ken vowed never to fight again. His, "mates", did try to get him into fights. A month after mickey, Ken and two mates were on their way home from school. They followed the well-worn path that cut through some old fields. It was a short cut from the three-mile trek that took you by the roadside to Ken's bus home. Ken's friends went off after a while towards were they lived. As Ken went over the crest of a hill, one of his mates, Pete was waiting for him alongside a kid who was a year younger than Ken. Ken knew of the kid, he'd come to the same junior school as himself a year or two after Ken. Ken knew he was a bit of a soft kid," Jimmy wants to fight you Ken". "No, no, no", Ken said, "never, but Jimmy threw two punches at Ken. Well they wouldn't have knocked the skin off a rice pudding. Ken threw a half powered right to the side of Jimmy's face and he fell to the ground. Ken waited a minute, then helped Jimmy to his feet. The ironic thing was, one year later, in the same place, the same patch of ground the same two were there. Pete, who still was one of Ken's best friends said, "Since last year Jimmy's been to boxing and judo lessons". Jimmy took up his boxing stance and strode forward, he threw a right and a left in quick succession. Ken dodged out of them, he could have delivered a quick uppercut to Jimmy's chin, however he backed off. Jimmy with fists clenched hit the defenceless Ken twice on the belly. Ken without thinking unleased a thunderbolt straight to jimmy's face, he fell backwards onto the ground with blood from his nose and lips running down onto his clean white shirt. Ken wished he could run away. Would it be an ambulance job, would he be up in front of the school for bullying? Jimmy sat up and said, "I'm never fighting again", he was alright, a good lesson he had learned. A relieved Ken got Jimmy to his feet, shook his hand, gave him a hug and helped to wipe the blood up. Pete strolled off on a different path. Again, Ken vowed never to fight again, probably through fear, he kept away from any arguments in school and, from any fighting.

The one and only time Ken's fists appeared again was at his sister Mary's eighteenth birthday party upstairs in the Tramshed Inn in Ramsvale. One guy, an uninvited guest was causing trouble at the bar. Ken approached the bloke who had been asked to leave, due to his bad mouth and behaviour. Ken asked him to leave, it was the usual response from half-drunk men. "Or what will you do?" Then a thrown punch at Ken, followed by a smart right hook from Ken that floored the fella. The next time ken saw that same person he was walking down towards ken on the same side of the road as Ken was walking up. When the two were some 100 yards apart Ken crossed the road, thankfully the other person carried on. As they passed each other, both gave a half salute. Ken was relieved, in fact extremely glad, as the fella must have put in two years of work at the gym and looked twice as big as he'd remembered. There would not be a punch thrown after that, NO WAY! Ken was married to his sweetheart at the age of 21. They had three children, two boys and a girl.

Throughout the whole of his marriage Ken never mentioned to his loving wife, and adorable kids, the times when his iron fists got him in, or out, of trouble. The scraggy kid, who never weighed more than 8stone in his life, continued to be a happy yet quiet, unassuming man. Ken taught his children never to argue or fight. He explained what the consequences of fighting could be, both physically and mentally.

Doug The Frog

There is a magnificent house in Gruby, which HAD a beautiful glorious watery haven in its wide and well-tended garden boundaries. The large reflective surface of the heavenly lake was a miracle of changing faces throughout the seasons. As mother nature's internal temperature started to rise and melt the icing on the cake that was snow and ice, the first visitors to its shores would appear.

A mother heavily pregnant, the father clinging on to protect his family. They reached the clear lapping waters and triumphantly entered into the crystalline depths. Shortly afterwards the clump of translucent jelly with black dots evenly distributed was clearly visible just below the flat surface of the water.

In that green and pleasant garden, frogs had lived and spawned in the lake for hundreds of years. That is until fifteen years ago. Five years before that the master of the mansion had passed over to a new heaven. The mistress of the house, unable to look after the exquisite but extensive grounds had to have the lake filled in. Now, where the tadpoles, insects and mayflies started out on their lives was a tract of land that was manicured grass lawn. There was no sign of a shallow cutting that could hold water. For years and years Frogs returned to that green carpet that covered the old lake. A dozen frogs each year aimlessly depositing their eggs.

On the ninth year one small rounded translucent ball had rolled behind a stone and rested in a small wet hollow with its little black dot of an embryo intact. In early Spring, with the temperature rising the little miracle was born and flourished.

That Spring and Summer the new born frog was nourished by natures abundant blessings of flora and fauna, and our frog journeyed far and wide, enjoying his life and gaining

Enjoying his life and gaining knowledge from what he saw and heard from humans, and various forms of animals and creatures. For the cold winter months, he hibernated deep under coverings small twigs, leaves and tree debris in the ground, well hidden from any disturbance, human, bird or rodent.

Our amphibious friend woke on an early mild sunny March morning. The sky was blue, blackbirds, robins, thrush and wrens were singing heavenly blessings. Daffodils and crocus were swaying in the light breeze. While skirting the perimeter of the garden our frog noticed what looked like a dozen or more armoured tanks in the distance. They were heading towards the site of the old lake. As they approached our friend, he counted twelve female frogs with twelve male frogs clinging tightly onto the females backs. "Go back and find some other pool because this one has been grassed over". "No", said the lead frog, "We are following what has been done for ages, it's our instant, and it is right". "You will not see one new life from your spawn, it is to no avail", spoke our frog. The lead frogs brushed aside our friend and marched on, only to be confronted by a huge seagull, who landed in front of them. "I have learned to change my life", said the seagull, "for the better, it's no longer humdrum, hunting for scraps on tips, or pinching food from seasiders' hands or mouths. I had a realisation and flew higher and wider than any other bird, to relax on the air currents and know when to dive down for my fish meal. Take notice of this young frog, he will lead you to good pasture and calming water. You and all who follow will be renewed in body and spirit. The lead frog ignoring seagull strode past him shouting, "I am off to lay my eggs, to reproduce, to help frog kind. Seagull warned the obstinate frog, "Come back you foolish and stubborn one". The frog walked on, seagull then picked up the frog in his beak, raised it up high dropped it into his mouth and gobbled it up. Seagull walked up to our friend and said, "Lead your people out of ignorance". He then flew off, up into the bright blue sky above a small cloud and out of sight.

The eleven remaining frogs, seeing their leader betray the wise seagull turned to our friend, who was now sitting on a mound of earth nearby. "We are all ready to lay our eggs, but there is no pond or pool for miles." Do not worry, see the Spring flowers, they each year follow natures course and give pleasure to all who see their grandeur. You have asked to be shown a better way, you know the old way is no longer, unless you and your offspring want to perish. Come, follow me, I will lead you out of this place".

The one who the seagull had said follow, and now the one who the lost frogs hapless frogs looked to, sedately walked down to the frogs, turned and started to jump in an easterly direction towards the high and very solid concrete fence. With all assembled at the fence one frog remarked, "We cannot get through the fence and so our eggs will perish here". Oh, ye of little faith ", our wise friend said, as he rolled back a rounded stone to reveal work that he had done before, there was a six-centimetre hole (about 3 inches in diameter). Each pair of frogs squeezed down into a short tunnel beneath the foundations of the wall and emerged into a new world; the neighbours garden. "The little frog must have dug that hole", said one of the male frogs. "Yes, because the frog has no name we should call him Doug, without his digging we would have had no hope of spawning", replied the female.

This garden was the opposite of their tidy place next door. It was like a tip, where anything not wanted from the house or other peoples was thrown into this narrow but very long garden. There were old bicycles, cupboards, mattresses, toys, rusty metal objects, all sorts of rubbish. The frogs looked dejected. "Come over here our newly named friend Doug commanded. Doug climbed up a broken old wooden fence and pointed to the side of a large blue plastic paddling pool, which lay about half a metre, (a foot and half), on top of other rubbish. "This year you can lay your eggs in here", Doug said. "That plastic is too slippery to climb up, it's impossible", remarked one of the frogs. "Not if one pair of you climbs on the other's shoulders", Doug said. He then stood on his hind legs with his body flat against the side of the plastic pool with his arms stretched out. "Climb on top of me". One pair did so, and then another on top of them, like a small ladder. Each frog pair in turn climbed up and over the edge of the pool, making a slash as they hit the welcoming water. The last two pairs were helped up by Doug pushing at the bottom, and frogs in the pool hanging over the edge and pulling the two remaining pairs up and over into the pool.

Doug roamed around to the other side of the new-found pond and climbed up a small twig onto the top of the pool, the twig breaking just as Doug made it, and he saw it fall down to the ground below. "You are safe here to swim, the pool is covered with moss and lichen having been here for years, and is safe from predators, too slippery to climb up and protected with shade from trees nearby, so birds can't see when flying over the site. However, you and all the tadpoles that make through froglet stage into full amphibians will be able to slide down and move from the pool. I will return at the end of the Summer, then I will lead all who want to leave this garden of rubbish on a journey to a place which you'll find is even more beautiful and safe than the one your grandparents and ancestors called home.

John & Joan

John and Joan are both in their eighties now, they've been married sixty-one years. John worked at the council as a gardener; a simple life, apart from the grave digging, especially in the pouring rain with the sides of the grave collapsing as the waterlogged soil pushed against the wooden boards on each side, putting pressure on the wooden struts that kept them in place, and the six feet deep hole intact.

John had many good days with fellow workers, learning about life and even the knowledge of trees and plants. The fulfilment of seeing flower beds, arrangements of plants and trees all looking beautiful after the hard work, gave the town an air of respectability, charm and character.

Joan had joined the council a few years after John, who had come straight from his courses at Screyin agricultural college with his certificates in horticulture and forestry. Joan came straight from Lanchester university with her first-class degrees in Business and business management, which put her in good stead for her job in the accounts department. With the easiness of her nature she became good friends with many work colleagues, as she gained promotions in her department. She had a good social life, with nights out and weekends away with her friends.

John and Joan first met at the annual Christmas Dinner and Dance for council employees. Sat across from each other the look, the smile, that special knowing, that yes! The evening passed by so quickly, a few dances together, then sitting next to each other, their spirits lifted, lots of talking and also periods of quiet serenity. The look into each other's eyes, drowning in happiness and bliss, in that magic place called love. Both had been the week before to Melcaster Arena to see Simply Red, they hadn't seen each other then, both were with a different group of friends. As the first chords of the final song, "You make me feel brand new", came across the dance floor; without a word, hand in hand, then in close embrace for the song, they left the dance floor, collected their coats and walked out of the council building. Not a word had they spoken to each other, as they floated on a cloud from heaven out into the biting cold of a December night. That Christmas day they got engaged, five months later on a beautiful sunny day in late May they were married.

The marriage proved to be a very happy and fulfilling one. Although no children had been born to them, they fostered many children up to when they reached their mid-fifties. They both retired at the age of sixty with good pensions and savings in the bank.

Twenty-five years later, and the couple were getting ready to drive back from their caravan in Criccieth North Wales to Silverglade Village on the north west coast of Lancashire. As they set off in their small car, Joan switched the radio on, the first song that came on was, Simply Red's, "You make me feel brand new". Both of them happy, smiling and singing the words together. Other well-known songs followed, and John and Joan sang their hearts out with actions and facial expressions making the journey a joy. The radio was turned off when the reception became poor, and a peaceful quiet ensued. Joan turned to john,

"You make ME feel brand new each day, all my life your love has kept me in happiness, you are the most loving precious love". John with a full heart and knowing mind answered, I'm at that stage in my life where I don't desire anything but to be with you Joan". Joan with a blissful countenance replied, "And me with you".

They stopped at Clandidno for a spot of lunch and to stretch their legs after the meal. Back in the car, John at the wheel, Joan glancing down at the Daily News said, "I bought a Lotto ticket", John replied, "That's the first one for two years". Joan said, "I don't know why I bought it, I just had a feeling, perhaps it'll be lucky. We don't need any money now, we don't need anything. If we win, we can give the money to people in genuine need". Later heading onto the M6 motorway John switches the radio on and tunes into Radio Lancashire. The first song played is played is Simply Reds, "You make me feel brand new". "Great", John says, "I'm so happy in love". Joan says, "I'm so happy I've spent my life with you, every day, every minute, every- "Barely two seconds with his eyes off the road, both glancing across at each other, John didn't see the large supermarket wagon in front come to a sudden stop behind a line of cars. The small car was a write-off with the two passengers killed instantly. Eventually John and Joan's bodies were taken to Creston crematorium. The assembly room was packed, and there were as many people outside the doors who could not squeeze in to the hall. Though there was no immediate family, many who had been friends of John and Joan and other loving people came to give their respects.

The small car that they had driven and enjoyed for the last seven years was inspected by the police, then with the insurance people, and was then picked up, craned onto the back of a pickup truck and taken to Snappers breaking yard in Notbowl.

Meanwhile one of Snappers workers Geoff, had found himself looking after his three children, aged six, seven and nine for the last twelve months. His wife Sharon had become increasingly dependent on alcohol. After years of problems between them, Sharon had gone down to Somerset to live with her elder sister. The last twelve months had been hard for Geoff. He liked a beer with his mates after work, but now he had to go straight home. Then it was time to prepare tea, (meal), and spend time with the kids. Now without his wife he was turning up at school late to pick the kids up. He now had to not only finish work early, but to drop the kids off in the morning. Geoff dropped them off as early as the school permitted, and then dashed off to work. Looking after a home, taking care of three children and working soon took a toll on Geoff. He was very tired. First of all, his boss warned him of his shorter days at work. His neighbours heard of his plight and took over the morning shift from 7:30, then later dropping the kids and their only child off at school.

The sadness of his marriage breakup, the rapid changes in his life, the depression and tiredness were changing this family man. In the mornings walking to work he'd consume two cans of beer. Soon it was noticed by fellow yard workers who gave him a shoulder to lean on and time to talk, hoping this would clear his head and he'd return to being the old Geoff again. It hardly worked, Geoff was

hauled in front of the boss, who suspended him for a
fortnight from work.

For the two weeks sabbatical his boss had given him £100
to tide him over, this respite was just what Geoff needed.
He rested up, hate better and healthier, and went for walks
in the local countryside while the kids were at school. By
the end of the two weeks Geoff's house, family and himself
were in great shape. He was pleased with himself, he felt
fitter, lost a few inches off his belly and was eager for a
return to the yard, to be back at work with his friends.

Geoff woke just as the previous day's and night's rain had
ceased. He walked to work on a beautiful clear blue sunny
June morning. He looked back on his time of depression
and drinking in the breakers yard with all the dangerous
work alongside and overhead of him, where a slip by him
could have cost a life, or at least injured someone who
would have to have time off work. All this he related to the
boss, they shook hands. The boss saw the changes in the
eyes and attitude of Geoff. "Welcome back Geoff, now get
that mountain of cars over there sorted out".

Geoff had been surprised to see the boss in so early,
although he shot off somewhere straight away in his blue
BMW 5series. Two other men were in before Geoff.
George, (Judd), who was on the crane, the main driver for
that for the last five years. The other man was Ralph, a wiry
but tough chap with a weather beaten wrinkled face that
appeared to hold a smile for most of the day. Ralph had
worked at Snappers for 25 years and he'd opened the gates
of the yard for the last seven years. He was driving the
"bulldozer", and shouted to Geoff, "Hiya kid, good to see

you back", --"I've squashed a lot of your vehicles in from
front and back, just take the front seats out, the dash and
anything else that is worth keeping". Geoff was deep into
his work, he'd cleared eight in the first two hours. Those
eight being loaded into the squasher one by one and
reduced to the size of a box. The next car, a small green
vehicle, no doors on of course. Geoff slackened off the
bolts that held the seats that had been damaged in what
appeared a head on smash. The dash and all else were gone
beyond any repair, he threw the seats aside. Only scraps of
a newspaper, a business card, a few extra strong mints in a
wrapper and a squashed and bent plastic bottle littered the
floor of the car. Geoff gathered the few items up in his
hands and went towards the litter bins as Ralph scooped up
the wreck to take it to the squasher. Geoff turned the pages
of the torn newspaper to see any interesting news or to see
the date, maybe of the day of the crash. Flicking the pages
over he found a half-folded piece of paper, yes! It was a
lotto ticket. "Aaah", Geoff smiled "good luck to whoever
was in the car; poor souls, did the person or people die, or
did they survive?" he wondered. He put the ticket and the
business card in the back pocket of his overalls, checked
the rubbish again and threw it into the trash bin, the plastic
bottle in the recycling bin.

On arriving home from work Geoff took his overalls off.
He fished out his loose change, a couple of oily rags, and
his wallet from his back pocket. As he did so the lotto
ticket fell to the floor. Geoff picked it up and put it on the
sideboard under his wallet. After getting the kids to bed,
Geoff settled down in his comfy armchair with a cup of tea
and switched the TV on. Minutes later he remembered the

lotto ticket, he just thought he might as well see if there was anything to come off it. He reached for it and with the remote moved to on demand and Lotto History. The lotto numbers for April 7th came up, Geoff wrote them down, and then opened the folded ticket. -4,5,9,23,26,48, B17. "Number 4 yep, 5 oh got those two, at least a free lucky dip that's good. Number 9-yeah- 23, 26 good, good God. A pause, then last one number 48, 48 48! Forty-Eight! Aaaaah ,-Geoff looked again,--Yes yes, oooh.Yes yes yes Whooooo!" Geoff shouted at the top of his voice. Seconds later his nine-year-old shouts down, "Are you alright dad?" ---"Yes, just watching something daft on the tele, goodnight". "Goodnight dad".

Geoff didn't sleep many hours that night. The one and only person with six numbers was Geoff, with the ticket that was worth £12.4 million pounds.

Geoff was an honest chap and over the next week his thoughts were everywhere. "Is the money mine, does it belong to a survivor of the crash, or if no survivors it means the money should go to the next of kin or some relative. What to do!? Geoff hadn't told a soul yet, not even his best mates at work or his neighbour. He would give them all a sizeable sum, problem was snappers would lose all its best men, and his neighbours would certainly all move from their terraced houses in Middle Darcy, away from where he was born and brought up in the village. Geoff decided to take things slowly. However, he thought, "No one knows, and even if they did would they object to me having some extra money for the house, kids and a holiday?" He rang the number on the ticket. The following week, as Geoff didn't want any publicity, although he did agree to saying the winner lived in Notbowl. Bank accounts were opened for him in London and in Meads in Yorkshire. He didn't want any financial advice or shares on the stock market.

On the Monday morning after seeing the children depart with the neighbour, Geoff dragged his old blue overalls over his steel toe capped boots and up his strong legs, over his shoulders and fastened the black buttons at the front. He picked up his Torrasays supermarket plastic bag with a sandwich and drink in. He strode over to the sideboard, put his loose change in his front pocket, and put his wallet in his back pocket, or so he tried to, it wouldn't go right in. "Let's see", he pulled out the bent-up business card. "Let's have a look", Nathaniels Ladies and Gents Hairdresser. 24, Western Street, Silverglade, Lancashire, and the telephone number. Geoff put it in his wallet and walked out of the door towards his work at Snappers.

Although Geoff had been taking small amounts of money from the bank to make life easier, he was still haunted by the fact that someone somewhere was undoubtable the true benefactor of the lotto money. All Geoff knew up to now was that the ticket was found in a small green car, a Nissma, and the address on the hairdresser's card, possibly the person lived in Silverglade.

The log book would have been sent through from Snappers office to Swansea by now. Would anything be still on Snappers computer? Could be! With everyone busy up the top end of the yard Geoff walked past the office windows. He knew the boss was on holiday, and Gerard who was in charge was with the guys in the bottom yard. Geoff strode into the office, went to the computer that stored the log details of all vehicle coming into Snappers and looked slowly through the dates. He found it, Green Nissma Niche, owner John Flacson, home address number 10, Magnolia Avenue, Silverglade. Geoff wrote the details down on a piece of paper and slipped out of the office. He looked across to the glass fronted building, the little café, where the workers, and the public who came in for parts for their cars could get a cuppa, breakfast or freshly made sandwich. Two ladies worked the café between them, Sara did most of the cooking and Tessa most of the waiting on tables and serving. It was nosy Tessa who Geoff saw looking at him as he came out of the office and turned to his right.

He acknowledges Tessa's wave by raising his left arm, and giving a knowing half nod to her, muttering under his breath, "It would have to be her, "Tell-tale Tessa". "Ah well nothing wrong in going into the office". Geoff then threw himself into his work with great vigour. He stopped for a brew for ten minutes and rang John Flacson's number on his mobile 'phone twice, each time he got no ringing tone, just a buzzing.

In the early evening after his tea time meal he tried again, same result, couldn't get through. Three weeks earlier he'd switched his gas, electric, mobile and got a home 'phone line with broadband put in, from the UK's leading utility company. For the first time he rang off his home 'phone, same buzzing. He then rang the operator; the end result was the line had been disconnected. Oh, has John Flacson moved, or, was he killed in the crash? Running out of hope he rang the hairdressers in Silverglade; the 'phone just rang and rang, no body there! Oh no, I'm not getting any nearer, is it worth trying to contact anyone? Geoff retired early to bed at 9pm, just after he'd put the kids to bed.

While having his twenty minutes lunch break with two good work mates, Geoff looked at them. How hard they worked in such an unclean and at times dangerous workplace. They were great fella's, both in their forties like him, how long could the three of them carry on in the yard, hopefully another ten years, and then what? Geoff decided if he kept the £12 million he'd put money in for the half a dozen fellas to receive it at the age of 55. Ralph and Jed were both around sixty, so he'd have to think about that later. It was raining cat's and dog's as they came out of the café. Geoff had plenty of work to do undercover in one of the open sided sheds. He fished the business card from his wallet and rang Nathaniels Haircutters. Two rings then, "Hello, Nathaniels Hairdressing Salon, Tracy speaking". - Geoff was stuck for words, "Err, I rang yesterday but…". "Closed all day Monday sir, would you like to book an appointment?" Geoff stammered, "I-err"-then a lightbulb moment, "have you anything after lunch this Thursday?"

The week before his neighbours had volunteered to take his three children this Thursday to Westport for the day. Geoff had sorted the kids out, given them some spence and put £300 in the hand of his close neighbour Mick, "Don't give me any back, enjoy yourselves".

Geoff was filled with anticipation, yet excited at getting to meet someone who had cut John Flacson's hair, and no doubt knew something about him. The Silverglade area Geoff knew reasonably well from trips with his wife and children, nice walks by the sea and through the forests. He went straight to the little village street that had one public house, two small grocery stores that sold newspapers, a by the seaside shop that sold everything from a bucket and spade to decent clothing and footwear for both summer and winter. He stopped outside the pub, where half a dozen well-heeled couples, possibly in their late twenties, were enjoying the sun, a chat and a drink, and asked for directions to the hairdressing salon. "Turn right at the end of the street, down the hill, keep left and that's Western street, where the hairdressers is some 50 yards farther up". Geoff turned right and saw a place to park down a street on the right. He was twenty minutes early, so he slowly walked down, watched the sea rolling in, and then walked to Nathaniels.

Geoff pushed the door open, ting-a-ling, a bell rang above his head. "Won't be a minute luv", a man shouted, "Take a seat". "Mr. Geoff?"- "Yes that's me". "Follow me". Tracy washed Geoff's hair, though he'd washed it that morning. She dried it a little and wrapped a white towel around it. "Sit here Geoff, Nat will be with you in a minute".

"Good Day Geoff, I'm Nat, now how would you like it cut", he said as he held Geoff's hair at the back. "If you'd cut it short at the back, and a good trim all round please". It'll be a pleasure Geoff". -The cutting started. "You booked a few days ago on the 'phone, how did you know about us?" I was sorting out some drawers at home, which I hadn't touched since my wife left me twelve months ago. I threw a load of old bills and stuff out, saw your card, and it reminded me of the times I'd spent in this area with my wife and young children. I remembered meeting a man up here years ago, John Flax or something his name, he gave me three cards, one where to stay, one good place to eat, and my hair must have looked in need, as he put your card with the others". Geoff added, "Did John Flax-on, I think that was it, did he come here?" "His name was John Flacson- FLACSON, yes he popped in now and again for a tidy up. His wife Joan we saw regularly, once or twice a month. They were a lovely couple" The word, "were", hit Geoff. - "Both were tragically killed in their car, after a holiday, on the way home up here" "I'm so sorry to hear that", Geoff said, "It must have been awful for their family, how old would their children be Nat?". "They were in their eighties Geoff, they didn't have any children, but they led a marvellous life helping others". - "How's that Geoff", Nat said as he showed Geoff the back and sides of his haircut through a mirror. "Absolutely brilliant Nat, many thanks". He shook Nat's hand and went and paid at the desk leaving a £5 tip. "See you", Geoff said, the same was echoed by Nat and Tracy. Geoff left the hairdressers feeling smart with the haircut and happy now he'd done all he could for the Flacsons, he was relieved and went to see the Flacsons old house.

Geoff soon found Magnolia Avenue, by walking north along the shore. The first houses, Nos 2,4 and 6 had long front gardens reaching down to the path that girded the shoreline. The houses were of modest single-story brick build of around the 1950's. No.8 had a ground floor and a 1st floor. This house was of a more recent build around the 1990's. The fifth house No.10 was situated as the path turned inward from the sea. The front of the house was facing north. This house was on the last two plots of Magnolia street. The front garden was hedged by a modern white plastic fence about five feet high, with a gate in the middle. There were hydrangea bushes and a Magnolia tree in the far corner. The garden was awash with cottage type flowers, and then---This two-story house had a roof garden. It was a beautiful modern house, yet with bay windows, it had an old style colonial feel. The house gleamed in the sun and looked like it had been built recently, possibly in the last year. There was assign on a post showing above the fence; it read: For Sale, Contact METTERS and Co., Estate Agents, Lanchester, followed by their 'phone number.

Geoff walked a couple of yards and sat down on a rock looking out to sea. Half an hour must have passed before he turned around and phoned Metters and Co. Geoff first inquired of the price, and who is selling the property. "Oh dear, was it a relation of John and Joan Flacsons?" Well he had to know. "I had met Mr. and Mrs. Flacson and I know they were killed in a car crash this year". - "I can tell you sir the proceeds of the house sale are split into three charities. The Flacsons won £10 million on the lotto two years ago. In their will they gave money to many friends, as well as some charities. They had no living relatives, so the will was simple. However, I believe Mather and Mather Solicitors still hold monies for three people who they are trying to trace, if you think you are one of them I'll give you the solicitors number.

After Geoff heard, "They had no relatives; tears flowed down his cheeks like water down a waterfall, and hearing the will was settled made him very emotional. He said, "Goodbye you've been a great help". He spoke a few final words and ended with a thank you and put the 'phone back in his pocket.

He sat down again on the rock and sobbed unceasingly for some five minutes. He came around looked at the surroundings, looked out to sea and then seemed to be lifted into a peaceful joyous heaven. An hour passed, and he felt a chill come over him, he lay for a while just out of the sea breeze, feeling secure, happy and blessed he went slowly and peacefully to sleep.

Some hours later, a couple on a stroll saw his body half hidden by a bush. They looked at each other. "Oh my God". "Who do we 'phone ", said the man as they grew closer.

As he got close to the, "body", he accidentally stood on a stick which made a loud noise as it cracked in two. The lady was just stretching out her arm to the body, when the, "corpse" reacted to the loud crack, and abruptly turned and lifted its head, "Whaaah, What the flipping eck", Geoff retorted. The woman shrieked, "Aaaah", and fell back onto her husband, who landed on the soft ground with his wife on top of him. Geoff got up, "Are you two alright", "Fine, fine", they said." I'd dozed off, had a hard day or two, thanks, and, see you take care".

It was nearly five pm, Geoff rang his neighbour, they were still in Westport having their fish and chips in Shark's café. All was well, Geoff had fish and chips at the pub in the village, and then drove home on a cloud.

The next week Geoff continued working, and sorting things out for the family and friends, though yet unknown to them. Geoff had promised the three children a holiday and took them up to the seaside town of Lessercombe for a fortnight. One day they drove the short distance up to Silverglade.

The kids played near the sea, had fish and chips in the garden of the pub, and then had a short walk on a path through a wood. They came down near the shore, on the path past the first four houses on Magnolia Avenue (grove). Geoff said to his children, "Do you like it up here in Silverglade". "Yes, yes", the two youngest said together, "We want to stay". The eldest, now age ten said, "It's beautiful, I'd love to live here". "Follow me ", Geoff said. They turned the corner, went up to the white gate and Geoff opened it. "Hold hands kids, welcome to your lovely garden, and…your new house.

And with that Geoff turned the key to the door of No. 10 Magnolia Grove and the four of them entered.

Thought For The Day

"Come fly with me", sang Frank Sinatra, (and Bubble), when they fancied a trip to Bombay or down to Acapulco Way.

Today the majority of people in this country have flown by some kind of aircraft. We've taken to the skies, in that mode of transport, the metal bird, and left the world down below for a while. But this is not the only way that man can fly. Man can fly without any mechanical aid!

Remember back in our childhood days, how we wondered at the flight of birds of the air. The sheer elegance of the butterfly, and the graceful humble bumblebee. Who according to scientists, should not be able to hover above the flower heads picking up the pollen because, it's body weight is too much for those tiny wings. I hope no one tells them, anyway they have a job to do, so on they go.

Remember our comic book heroes like superman, who had incredible powers, including being able to fly just about anywhere. Like myself, you may have laid in bed at night, or daydreamed lying down in the fields, that you could glide over hills and dales, and swoop down low over field and hedgerow, then accelerate, turn to one side and shoot down between tall trees, and up again into the great blue yonder. How great that was! Later disappointment, man cannot fly the teachers proclaimed, yet they would read us stories of fairies and angels! Even if you saw these beings yourself, you were told you were imagining the whole episode! Angels are real but, they are UP in heaven! At catholic secondary school we were all taught we had a guardian angel. We were taught the miracles of Christ and those of the Apostles. Ahh, the fire was kindled again, I knew it, man can do anything, it is all within us, each one of us, YES!

In all the world's religions there are references to flying. In our Christian way we read of Christ Jesus, "He led them out as far as Bethany, then he blessed them, and was carried to Heaven". Joseph of Cupertino: In 17 recorded cases he was suspended for hours or balanced in the branches of a tall tree. One time he took others up with him. Once he cured a man with a mental illness, by dragging him up into the air by the man's hair. A handy chap to have around if you have a cat that gets stuck up in high places! St. Theresa of Avila had to be held down on occasions. Theresa wrote of her experiences: The mind draws the body up with a sweet experience of bliss, Theresa was free of gravity though aware of her body. St. Francis of Assisi, often seen hovering around the monastery with such radiance, humble and at peace long before the hovercraft was invented. St. Seraph of Russia, St. Maria of Agrilla both floated in the air from A to B. St. Dominic lifted up in 1601 in the court of the King and Queen of Spain.

In England Miriam Bradley often flew up and sat on the highest branch of the linden tree. Douglas Home was seen flying by both a Nobel prize winner and the Count Tolstoy. When sitting he'd rise up with his chair. All we seem to need to enjoy the freedom from gravity, and the joy and bliss that goes with it, is has Christ Jesus said: The innocence of a child and the purity.

So, the next time you sit quietly in your favourite chair, nice and relaxed, and slip into that quiet state of awareness where all things are possible, be prepared, because YOU could be in Acapulco before Frank Sinatra, or Bubble, have fastened their seat belts!

To
Danny & Lesley,

Thank you for being
true friends always.

John

Printed in Great Britain
by Amazon